ENZO'S MAMMA

To Kathy,
Because you always
have a bright smile...
Enjoy this Italian escape.
Wendy
Ramo
10/18/06

Kathy,

So that yo always
have this fragit Smile...
with this Thelion.

love
Jane
10/8/06

ENZO'S MAMMA

Wendy Ramer

iUniverse, Inc.
New York Lincoln Shanghai

ENZO'S MAMMA

iUniverse books may be ordered through booksellers or by contacting:

iUniverse
2021 Pine Lake Road, Suite 100
Lincoln, NE 68512
www.iuniverse.com
1-800-Authors (1-800-288-4677)

This is a work of fiction. All of the characters, names, incidents, organizations and dialogue in this novel are either the products of the author's imagination or are used fictitiously.

ISBN-13: 978-0-595-40782-8 (pbk)
ISBN-13: 978-0-595-85146-1 (ebk)
ISBN-10: 0-595-40782-X (pbk)
ISBN-10: 0-595-85146-0 (ebk)

Printed in the United States of America

For Marc,
For introducing me first to Bologna and then to motherhood

Acknowledgments

So many thanks go out to the following people: Karyn Krause Amore, for her knowledge and her friendship; Jay Kreutzer, for his legal expertise in divorce law; David Abraham, for his creativity and legal expertise in immigration law; Barbara Goldberg, for being my first fan; and Marc Ramer, for his continuous love and encouragement.

P R O L O G U E

▼

Wrapped in a blue, imitation-fleece airline blanket, I cannot stop biting my nails. I am working on my left pinky with the vengeance of a woman who has held back her fears for far too long and is finally about to face them…which I am. This little nail is a tricky one to get to, so I combine the use of my incisors with the strength of my right hand. That pinky nail must go; it is only fair that it should match its four left-hand partners in crime. I may appear to be handling my task like a frustrated addict, but I've honestly never partaken in this habit before this flight. In fact, I've made this journey from Miami to Milan before—without nail-biting incident, but nine years have passed since my last return. A lot has happened in nine years. Considering the fact that I've managed to avoid cigarettes, drugs, and alcohol abuse, biting my nails seems an innocent vice to pass the time.

The pilot notifies us that we'll be arriving in three hours, and I commence work on my right index fingernail. Out of the corner of my eye, I notice the gentleman on the aisle seat opposite mine looking on with an expression of disgust mixed with pity. I can only imagine how the sight of a grown woman so voraciously indulging in this oral habit must look, but I don't give a damn. I still have five fingers to go.

PART I
CARLO

CHAPTER 1

▼

Twelve years ago, I landed in Bologna, Italy for the first time. I was twenty-two years old, fresh out of college, and ready to conquer the world...starting with Italy. My parents, Allan and Karen, had spoken of Bologna for as long as I could remember. They had spent a good portion of their early-married years in the historic university town, capital of the central northern region of Emilia-Romagna, and had, in fact, named both my sister and me in honor of the hilly, Italian province. I, Emilia (better known as Millie), was conceived in the damp, Etruscan-inspired city but born in Miami while my younger sister, Romina, came along two years later to complete the homage. Her nickname is Romy, leading others to assume that she was named for the famed Roman capital of Italy, but those dear to the Gossett family know better.

As for my world conquest, 1994 was unfortunately the beginning and the end because I never made it beyond Italy. But many would agree that conquering Italy and the Italians is a noteworthy feat. The only problem is that nobody can really conquer Italian men, except for the mamma, who has already accomplished that before an Italian boy is even old enough to flirt with a girl. So when a naively bold American girl crosses the Atlantic Ocean and succumbs to the Italian boy's charms, she is blindsided before she even knows what hit her.

Ah, the mamma. When I met Regina Buonsignore di Mazzini, I hadn't yet mastered enough Italian to realize that her given name, Regina Buonsignore, translated to "Queen of the Good Man." Had the case been otherwise, I would have at least been forewarned of her power over her son when I fell in love with him. Carlo was indeed a good man when he was twenty-three years old, but Regina had not yet exhibited the full force of her powers. That would have to wait until Carlo chose another woman to love. And that is where I enter the story.

It was lunchtime on the day after Carlo and I had consummated our relationship when I met the mamma for the first time. Regina Buonsignore was an attractive woman who had barely entered her fifties. Her light brown hair rested neatly on her square shoulders, and her hazel eyes were exactly the same as Carlo's. I found it amazing that the same eyes could convey such different messages when seen as the windows of two different souls, and I wondered what had happened to Regina that had hardened such beautiful eyes.

Her gaze practically burned me as Carlo and I entered the apartment. Although we had showered since our lovemaking, the scent of the moment still lingered, and the glow of new love was more evident than ever. It is for that reason (and the undeniable fact that Carlo had not slept at home the previous night) that I believe Regina received me into her home with such open hostility.

"Mamma, this is Emilia." He introduced me by my formal and—let's not forget—Italian name. I was sure this was done in an attempt to win Mamma over and forego emphasizing my American nationality. But it wasn't until she opened her mouth to speak that I realized what Carlo was really trying to overshadow.

"Yes, the Jew."

Not even a word of welcome and it was already out there. From that moment on, no matter what hint of kindness she might ever display, I would forever and always be the Jew. And then, when I thought Carlo was about to gallantly jump to my defense, I heard him say something even worse.

"She's only half-Jewish, Mamma. Her father was raised Catholic."

There are moments in life when true courage offers itself up on a silver platter for you to take a bite of, and it is that decision to either grab a helping or politely decline that reveals a person's strength of character. As I stood in Regina's kitchen and listened to my lover denounce my Judaism, I saw the server approaching me with the platter of courage. I felt my posture weaken as I secretly shook my head, watched the server do an about face, and walk away from me, carrying the platter full of my courage and my character. My eyes welled up with tears, though I'm still not sure if they were tears of shame, disappointment, or both.

"What is she doing?" The mamma threw out an open hand in exasperation. "Your girl meets me for the first time and cries? Am I so bad?"

I ran out of the kitchen and towards the bathroom, whose open door welcomed me much more sincerely than Carlo's mamma had. I closed the door behind me and sobbed as I listened to Carlo shout at his mamma. He said lots of things in Italian that I did not understand. She simply responded with that repetitive click of the tongue. "Tsk, tsk, tsk."

Carlo eventually coaxed me out of the bathroom. He firmly took me by the hand and led me out of the deadly quiet apartment and onto the noisy comfort of the street below. We walked in silence down his street and turned into a small piazza. Once out in the open, he released his grip on my hand and pulled me toward him for a hug.

"I'm so sorry," he said.

I said nothing, letting myself get lost in the comfort of his chest and the warmth of his arms. It was at that moment when I realized how similar the emotions of love and hate can be. In both cases, you care so much about the other person's well-being. On the one hand, you want nothing more than to please and comfort. On the other lies the driving desire to see your lover's hard downfall.

Carlo and I met in a church. (And here come the woulda, coulda, shouldas.) If the writing on the walls had been in English, I might have been able to read between the lines and find my fortune carved out for me right there in that small, beautiful chapel. I would have understood that the church would come to represent everything that was different about Carlo and me, and I could have escaped before he ever saw me and let the church come between us, leading to our demise. I could have turned around and pushed my way through the solid wooden doors and let the early autumn daylight awaken my senses with a crisp wind. But I didn't do that. Instead, I stayed inside the Church of Santo Stefano and allowed my senses to remain suppressed by the heavy scent of incense that burned too sweetly, inviting me to light a candle.

I think I'll remember that moment as long as I live, because even then, I felt guilty for what I was doing...silently reciting the blessing over the Sabbath candles as I lit the amber votive and then shielded my eyes with both my hands. That's the traditional way to light the Sabbath candles, and it also helped me avoid staring blankly at the large painting of the Virgin Mary that hung above the small altar. I was never a very religious person, but the sanctity of the church and the soft glow of the candlelight inspired me to pay my respects. After all, it was Saturday morning, Shabbat, and I thought God would understand. Whether Catholic, Jewish, or a little bit of both, as was my case, acknowledging the presence of God when in His home was the right thing to do. Did it matter that everyone else

who prayed there sent their prayers through His Son or the Blessed Virgin? I was going directly to the source, and I thought God would appreciate my efforts to find Him in that Catholic town. At the time, I actually interpreted the moments that followed my blessing as proof of God's appreciation. I believed He was sending me a gift in the form of Carlo Mazzini. Unfortunately, I had grossly mistaken a punishment for a present.

I had just finished my prayer and was letting my hands down when I realized that someone was standing next to me. Carlo was standing so close that my left shoulder brushed his right jacket sleeve when I flinched in surprise.

"Did I interrupt a private moment?" He asked in Italian as he smiled wryly.

"As if you didn't know," I responded in my best sarcastic tone...in English.

Carlo was disarmingly attractive and a good head taller than I was. His skin was the color of creamed coffee, and his hazel eyes were speckled with gold. His lean frame carried his Armani-like attire with elegance, and his chocolate-colored hair was just long enough to rest lightly on the collar of his caramel leather jacket. Despite my efforts to sound annoyed and confident, I was intimidated. Perhaps sensing my discomfort, Carlo dropped the smile and assumed the apologetic stance.

"Please forgive me," he responded in near-perfect English. "I was inappropriate and rude."

I nodded once in acknowledgment.

"I am Carlo. Could I please buy the beautiful American a cappuccino on this chilly morning?"

How could I resist? Yes, I hear you. The words would have been *No, grazie.* But I've always been a sucker for charm (still am), and instead of pronouncing that two-letter word that begins with "N", I feigned modesty at being called beautiful, smiled coyly, and said, "That would be a nice way to say you're sorry."

When two people are getting to know each other and the connection feels like a good fit, time enters a different dimension. I am not scientifically savvy, but I am sure there is some evidence to prove my theory. That proof comes in the form of real (or imagined) moments where words and facial expressions that would otherwise be taken as subtle nuances of communication turn themselves into slow motion sounds and images to be imprinted in the mind of each participant. Never again will either person remember conversational details with such precision nor offer their attention with such undivided focus. This can only happen because time has slowed down or, at the least, changed its form. In the normal world, it appears linear and is measurable by calendars and watches. But in the world of new love, time's only reminder is auditory; it can be heard in the change of the rhythm of the city streets, in the low rumble of a hungry stomach awaiting its next meal, and in the distant ringing of church bells.

After leaving the Church of Santo Stefano, Carlo and I headed up Via Santo Stefano to Via Rizzoli and wound our way through some smaller alleys before ending up at Gelateria Gianni, Carlo's favorite place for coffee and gelato—the Italian ice cream that puts its American counterpart to shame. Although the entire journey lasted no more than fifteen minutes, time had lost all meaning. Once outside the little church, Carlo's demeanor had changed dramatically. He was out of pick-up artist mode and into, what I could only imagine one might call There-Is-Something-Special-About-This-Girl-So-Be-Yourself mode. Even though Carlo had been very well educated in English, we alternated between his mother tongue and mine as I attempted to behave appropriately in my host country and practice my new-found skills but instead realized that not much could be accomplished socially in that fashion. Carlo was a patient escort and confessed to enjoying the sound of my English-speaking voice over the Italian version. I felt slighted at the back-handed compliment but decided not to take myself so seriously. Oh, how I now wish I had taken myself more seriously. But at twenty-two years old, how can a girl know?

The American ex-pat condition is unique. When foreigners come to live in the United States, their reasons are varied. Many come with the hopes of finding economic or social improvement, while others are running so fast from the political strife of their homeland that they plant their feet in American soil and, for once, exhale deeply. Historically, there has always been the group of immigrants that are fleeing persecution, believing that freedom of everything will save their souls in America. And occasionally, there is the visitor who comes for just that purpose, to visit and glimpse American life before returning home with a feeling of one-upmanship on friends and family, looking down on the American dream as nothing more than frothy legend. But the American ex-patriot is different.

Rarely do you find American citizens emigrating. Ironically, when Americans choose to reside in another country, possible reasons often mirror the sentiments of those who came to the States in the first place…political disillusion, social disappointment, and persecution from a societal construct that can be enslaving. The young ex-pat leaves the United States often with the simple intention of traveling or having a brief experience living abroad, but what often prevails is an extended love affair with an exotic or distinct lifestyle, one that soothes the internal struggle of the young American…the struggle with boredom. It is not until many years later, when the ex-pat has returned home (as most eventually do), that those same aspects of life that had once weighed the American down will now conjure a sense of comfort. But sadly, the bored soul will inevitably

resurface, and nostalgia for the foreign life lost seeps into the repatri-
ated American, fostering the never-ending need to remember,
whether good or bad, a part of life that once challenged the mundane.

If I had been able to steal a peek at my future, I am sure I would
have turned on my heels before allowing my impromptu coffee and
ice-cream date with Carlo to turn into a full day of strolling the city
streets, shopping at the Piazza Otto Agosto Flea Market, lunching at
a hidden trattoria, and strolling again until the September sun
began to drop below the horizon in perfect synchronicity with the
church bells, whose beautiful chimes rang high above the energized
city on that magical autumn eve. They were telling me that it was
time to go home…if only I had understood the true meaning of
home.

"So, what do you do with yourself when you're not out to conquer
the world?" Carlo had picked up on my over-achieving aspirations
and posed this question as we sat on a bench in Montagnolo Park.

"I'm not really out to conquer the whole world, you know." I
leaned in close to him as I whispered my response.

Carlo leaned in even closer. "Just my heart, right?"

Those are the kind of moments you remember, years later when
all the bad stuff clears from your head to allow the little details to
shine through.

I felt Carlo's body heat against my shoulder and took a deep
breath in an attempt to regain my composure. "In the mornings, I
do little more than sleep or wander around town." I tried to answer
Carlo's original question. "But don't think for a minute that I do it
aimlessly."

Carlo smiled and cocked his head as he surveyed me. "Something
tells me that you do very little in your life aimlessly."

"Having no real destination affords me the opportunity to happen upon some of Bologna's most hidden charms. Do you realize how many charms are hidden in this town of yours?"

"Tell me."

"I specifically choose to observe the things that others around me ignore…the things that go unnoticed to their unappreciative eyes."

"Like what?"

I wanted to tell Carlo about some of my discoveries, but their details seemed too arduous to describe while sitting so close to him. I wanted to tell him about the day I was strolling down Via dell'Independenza, a main north-south artery that originates in the city center, when I noticed a wooden panel, no larger than a small window, seemingly placed quite randomly in the middle of the wall. It had a handle that I could hear begging for my approach. So I did what the handle implored me to do; I pulled it open. I actually had to stand on tip-toes to see what lay beyond and below…a small surviving stretch of the Reno Canal. It ran right under the road on which I stood, and I would have sworn I was in Venice instead of Bologna. I later learned that in medieval times, the Reno was part of an expansive network of waterways that transversed Bologna and helped connect factories and mills to their sources of business.

I wanted to tell Carlo these fascinating details, but my thoughts sounded like words that would only pollute the air between us—air that we shared as we breathed in and out, gazing into each other's eyes.

"Like what?" Carlo asked again.

"Like the secret door."

"You mean the one that leads to your heart?" Carlo looked so serious that it made me laugh.

"Not exactly," I giggled. "The one that leads to the Reno Canal."

"What are you talking about?" He had no idea what I meant, but his eyes lit up at the thought of something secret and forbidden.

"My point exactly. When you live here, you don't see things that have always been there to see. I'll take you to the secret door some day," I told him, feeling rather proud of myself for knowing something about his city that he did not.

"I know how to find the Reno Canal," Carlo said. "Your heart is another story."

My afternoons were as educational as my mornings but in another manner. That was when I earned my keep in the two-bedroom apartment that I rented off Via D'Azelio by teaching English at one of two language academies that employed me. Those classes started at three o'clock and ran until six o'clock in the evening, when I would then grab the bus across town to make my night classes. The moonlighting job had me out on the town until 9:30, such that I usually arranged to meet a colleague or friend (often one in the same) for a glass of wine before returning home to my Italian roommate, Michela, a student at the University of Bologna, also known as the oldest university in the western world and Dante's alma mater. The university was also the place where Carlo Mazzini would be spending most of his time come October when classes resumed, studying for his degree in Computer Science, a field of study which Dante Alighieri's artistic mind would probably have never even fathomed could some day exist.

After a few weekends of romantic Saturday strolls mixed with some weeknight dinner dates and too many visits to Gianni's (made clearly visible by the extra five pounds I was sporting), Carlo and I had had enough of the niceties. Our good-bye kisses were passionate and delicious but no longer satisfying enough to suppress our deeper wants and needs. Knowing that Michela had gone to her hometown of Ravenna for the weekend and willing myself to ignore the church bells' cry to "go home," I led Carlo up the three flights of stairs to my quiet apartment and into my warm bed. He then led himself into me, and we loved each other with all the pent up passion that had been stored up since that day on Via Santo Stefano.

It was during lunch the next day when I met Regina for the first time and discovered that growing up in an interfaith environment had done nothing to prepare me for the religious wars that raged on foreign battlefields.

The weeks that followed what I affectionately refer to as the Meeting of the Mamma were tenuous. Carlo had greatly disappointed me, so I avoided returning his phone calls and even told Michela to answer the intercom when I was home, just in case Carlo should stop by. And he did, calling on me on several occasions and even yelling Italian obscenities of frustration at Michela through the intercom when she vehemently denied my being home. I did not know any other way to face my confusion. I felt helpless when I tried to imagine a future with Carlo. Our one night together had been the most magical thing to happen to me in my newly-established adult life, and I knew I had (rather too quickly) fallen in love with him. When I practiced the resolution in my mind, when I addressed the demon issue of my religion and how Carlo really felt about it, and even when I imagined the most acceptable of responses that Carlo could muster, it just didn't add up; there was always the mamma. I knew my generation was open enough to learn new ideas and adopt new attitudes despite all opposing upbringing, but I could in no way visualize Regina's acceptance. And she was the linchpin. So I continued refusing to face Carlo. I called my method of dealing with my emotions Avoidance...certainly not a creative approach to resolving problems but arguably the most common. Avoidance was the outright enemy of Confrontation, which was obviously Carlo's method of operation. Then, when I thought that things couldn't get worse, they did.

First, I must explain what happened to me when I was sixteen years old. I got my period for the first time. (*She's a late bloomer,* they all smiled lovingly.) But then it did not return until I was eighteen. The gynecologists ran their battery of tests and determined that I had very lazy ovaries. (*Thank God that trait hasn't carried over to her study habits,* they all smiled lovingly...again.) I was told that I would probably never have a regular menstrual cycle and would most likely never be able to conceive. I made it through four years of university with only four periods to show for it...one for each not-so-lazy year of hard work. As you can imagine, birth control was never my concern. In fact, my three college boyfriends thought my lack of reproductive ability was the coolest thing in the world; that is, until I requested they use condoms to prevent sexually transmitted diseases. But even that preventive practice eventually got old as we fooled ourselves into believing that knowing each other well precluded the need for protection against our pasts. So there I was in Bologna, without a care in the world or a condom, and in love with Carlo Mazzini.

The Christmas holidays were approaching, and I had successfully, for lack of a better word, broken up with Carlo. It was action through inaction. He seemed to have given up his attempts at winning back my affections, and I was looking forward to visiting my family back in Miami. I'd had an on and off again stomach bug through most of November, but it seemed to have run its course. When I arrived in Miami in mid-December, I fell ill once again. I blamed it on stress, but my mother encouraged me to see a doctor "while you're in a country with good medical care." It seemed that the Italians did not control the field concerning prejudice; that was fair game world over.

I sat in the cold examining room of Dr. Goldman's office, awaiting the results of a urinalysis. I didn't understand the need for one, but Dr. Goldman made the suggestion simply because I had been out of the country for awhile. He said it was a good diagnostic tool. Finally, he returned to my room and shut the door behind him.

"Miss Gossett," he began. "Do you have any reason to believe that you could be pregnant?"

I think I actually sputtered and coughed at the same time before I sarcastically responded. "With my lazy ovaries? I haven't had a period in over a year. I don't think so."

"I think you need to give your ovaries more credit than that," he said with a very serious tone. "You're pregnant."

Though my mouth froze, I could hear my own voice verbalizing the calculations in my head. Late September…what day was it exactly? October, November, December…almost Christmas Eve. "I'm more than 12 weeks—" I couldn't bear to pronounce the "P" word.

"And you've put on a few pounds since last year's visit," commented Dr. Goldman.

I muttered half out loud, half to myself, "I thought it was the gelato."

CHAPTER 2

▼

When you're twenty-two years old, you feel like you are part of the trunk of a large flowering tree. You haven't quite reached any branches yet, or if you have, you're only at the base of that branch, still giving you lots of wiggle room to determine your true direction. Which branch you will continue to grow into and which fingers of that branch you'll become have yet to be determined. You really won't flower until you've chosen your branch and traveled far enough out and have no where else to go but to the bud. You imagine yourself budding some time in your late twenties or early thirties and then holding strong as a beautiful flower for as long as you can. If you think about it long enough, you realize that eventually your flower will reach the end of its cycle and have no other choice but to fall from the tree and return to the earth.

Before my visit to Dr. Goldman's office, I saw myself solidly traveling through the trunk; I hadn't neared the point of choosing a branch. I was out to conquer the world, which included whichever branch I chose. After my medical visit, things looked very different. I sat on the beach on a clear day in late December and watched the white caps of the waves crest and fall and form again. I saw my tree of life. Suddenly, it had far fewer branches than I remembered. There were really only two for me to choose from: the one where I return to Bologna, confront Carlo, and try to make my life work with a child and hopefully with Carlo's support, or the branch where I terminate the pregnancy, never mention it to Carlo, and live with the forever memory that I might have ruined my one and only chance at having a baby. My decision had to be made immediately since I was already on the fringe of starting my second trimester.

I was raised in a household where I was always told that I could discuss anything I wanted with my parents. But how do you explain to the two people who love you more than anyone else that their words often did not match their actions. How do you tell them that sometimes, even at twenty-two years old, there are life decisions that must be made alone so as to not harbor any undeserved resentment towards those who helped you make that decision? If my parents convinced me to have an abortion and I came to regret the decision later, it would be too easy to hate them. And if they convinced me to keep the baby and I came to resent that child...too much hate. The only one I could afford to let down was myself.

I thought about that day when I was eighteen and was told that I would probably never conceive. Doctors certainly don't know everything. I thought about when I was a little girl and dreamed of having my own baby. My baby dolls were my most precious toys, so much so that I often became aggressive towards my sister if she tried to take one away from me. Even then, no one was going to take away my baby. Then I remembered the story of my own conception, which quite ironically occurred in Bologna, Italy. I laughed out loud until my laughter turned into sobs. And there I sat on that beautiful sandy beach, crying at the ocean, whose crashing waves sympathetically and mercifully drowned out my tears.

I spent the rest of my Miami vacation much to myself. My parents sensed that I was bothered by something, and when I wouldn't fess up, they decided that ignorance was bliss, proof that avoidance was an inherited trait.

As I flew the nine hours east over the Atlantic Ocean towards Milan, I formulated my plan of how to approach Carlo. I wanted this life in Italy, even if it wasn't the life I had originally envisioned. I carried a beautiful secret inside me, and in my fantasies, my secret would reveal itself in Italy, live a charmed life, and rescue me from self-doubt. So determined was I to make my own destiny that I had abandoned my country and my parents without leaving so much as a hint as to the source of my angst.

As the train zoomed by quaint town after quaint town on the two-hour journey between Milan and Bologna, I practiced my dialogue. I was sure that Carlo would take me back if we could just manage the mamma. And now that I was to become the mamma of his child, I was sure that my place in the Mazzini family would be solidified.

There is a word whose meaning is hard to define...sure. Are we ever really sure of anything? I'm sure that my name is Millie. (But it isn't; it's actually Emilia.) I'm sure that I was conceived in Bologna. (Why? Because my parents told me so? They could have miscalculated the date.) I'm sure that I'm pregnant. (Why? Because the doctor said so? Because I've put on few pounds? It could really have been the gelato.) The point is that I wasn't really sure of anything, except for my decision to not abort my pregnancy. Because I was in full support of a woman's right to choose, I felt rather proud of myself for my own choice. And I was grateful that I had the choice to make; hopefully, that would mean no regrets.

As the January frost chilled my feet even through my boots, I stood outside Café Zanetti, on the corner of Piazza Galvani and Via Farini. I was waiting for Carlo. Because Zanetti was one of Bologna's most well-known cafés, it was rarely a quiet place to be, and it was specifically for that reason that I had chosen it; I think I was looking for the crowd's protection. I could have gone inside, but the cold air blowing against my cheeks energized me. I hoped it would give me the courage I needed so badly. I had called Carlo the day before, much to his shock and pleasure it seemed, and invited him for a coffee. On the phone, I told him nothing more than that my vacation had given me the time and distance to think about him and how much he meant to me. His voice remained calm as he agreed to meet me, but his mispronunciation of some common English words allowed me to hear a mixture of excitement and trepidation.

If a stranger had been watching me while I awaited Carlo, he would have thought I was insane, muttering to myself and staring off at nothing. Actually, I was practicing my part in the dramatic role of the one who had to drop the bomb. Carlo would play the part of the unknowing innocent who would have to avoid perishing in the explosion.

When I saw Carlo approaching, I surprised myself with stomach flutters and the feeling that I was so stupid to have ever let him go. He greeted me with a wide smile, though I could see the tension in his brow. There was the awkward moment where neither of us knew if we should kiss, hug, or neither. In a split second, Carlo took the reigns and leaned in for a kiss on each cheek, and a warm hug. For one moment, I felt safe and that everything was going to be all right. When he released his embrace, he checked me out. No words passed between us, but I could see his eyes fixate on my thickened waist. I subconsciously wrapped my coat tighter around my abdomen, but Carlo's sparkling smile told me that I looked just fine. He opened the door to Café Zanetti and held out an arm to let me pass first.

"You look great!" Carlo's first words as we sat down at a table with our warm cups of coffee in hand. "In fact, Mamma would think you look especially wonderful now that you've put on a few extra pounds." He winked at me as he said, "Looks like you've been eating well back home."

"Carlo," I paused. "I actually haven't been eating much of anything lately. I can't seem to keep it down."

"Have you been ill?" He sounded genuinely concerned.

"No."

When I didn't offer further explanation, Carlo chose not to press. "So how were your holidays?" He asked in a casual, small-talk tone.

"Fine." I could feel my awkward smile tightening my cheeks, and I wondered if Carlo knew the difference between my lying smile and the genuine version. It had been months since we'd last seen each other, and we had really only known each other for a few weeks, intense as they were.

"Why exactly did you call me here if you really don't want to talk?" Carlo didn't sound angry as much as confused.

"I *do* want to talk."

Carlo nodded as he held both palms up to heaven and waited.

I surveyed the crowd and saw all types: families, couples, friends, business associates. You can tell a lot about people's relationships if you watch carefully. You just need a keen eye and a good imagination. Nobody was looking at Carlo and me, but I wondered what they would say about our relationship if they did. Even I was unsure of our relationship. But I had gambled on Carlo's confidence when I chose not to terminate my pregnancy, so I realized that I owed him more than curt, one-word responses. Time to drop the bomb. "Carlo, I'm pregnant." And then, only because he broke eye contact and looked down into his lap, I added, "Yes, it's yours."

I once thought that love and hate were frighteningly similar emotions. But sitting there with Carlo, I realized how remarkably identical silence and noise can be. Because of the silence between us, the noise of our surroundings became amplified so strongly that I had to put my hands in my lap in order to prevent myself from cupping them over my ears. The clanging of spoons against ceramic mugs and the screeching of the espresso maker grated my nerves to the point that I suddenly heard myself shout to Carlo, "Say something, please!"

He looked up at me immediately and asked, "Do you want to keep it?"

I nodded my head.

"Do you want me to be a part of your life?" He then asked.

That was a question I hadn't considered when I practiced my part. To me, it was obvious that I wanted him to be in my life, or else I would never have said anything. I could have stayed in the States, raised the child on my own, and never have involved myself with Carlo or his mamma again. "That's why I'm here," I told him.

He pondered the situation for a brief moment and then blew me away. "Then there is no question. I want you to marry me so we can be a family."

I put my hand to my mouth so that I could say nothing, because there really was nothing to say at that moment. Childhood fantasies usually die hard, if they ever die at all. But my reality was staring me in the face and effectively saying that whatever fantasies I had harbored about how I would get married or when I would start my family had just become history and perhaps even fodder for future therapy sessions. Finally, I found the breath to speak. "You really *want* to marry me?"

"Well," Carlo began. "Perhaps it isn't under the exact circumstances that I would have preferred, but I think I loved you from the first moment I saw you blessing your Sabbath candles."

"You didn't even know what I was doing," I chided.

"No, but I knew you respected God, and I knew you were beautiful."

"And what about the fact that I'm Jewish?" Now seemed the time to have the religion talk that was so long overdue.

"I find it interesting that you choose to call yourself Jewish when your father is a Catholic."

Things obviously needed to be laid out on the table in as clear a fashion as possible for this highly-educated but unworldly Italian. "Carlo, my father never identified with the Catholic Church when he was growing up. When he met my mother, he understood how important it was to her, as it is to most Jews, to preserve her culture, because for many American Jews, Judaism is more than a religion; it's their culture."

"Do you go to temple regularly back in Miami?" He challenged.

"You aren't listening," I scolded, trying not to sound as defensive as I felt. "It isn't so much the act of attending regular synagogue services that makes a person feel Jewish. It's the 5,000 years of history told and retold throughout Jewish upbringing in holidays like Chanukah, Purim, and Passover." I could almost see myself on my pulpit. "It's a history that we can't deny and are taught to preserve at all cost, lest we lose our identities and succumb to the Christian world that would probably prefer our complete assimilation anyway." Carlo was now listening intently, and I appreciated it greatly. So I continued. "My father had no problem sending my sister and me to Hebrew School to learn about our Jewish heritage because he knew that living in the United States would provide all the non-Jewish education we would need."

"And what about Christmas…didn't you miss it?"

I had to admit that his innocence was charming. "Since you mentioned it, during Christmas, we were actually lucky enough to have a Christmas tree lighting up the house along with the Chanukah menorah. And though I knew I was half-Catholic and half-Jewish, the world always seemed to focus on the latter, and eventually I did too."

"But now you live in Italy, where Jews are such a small number, especially in Bo. Don't you think it would be uncomfortable to be Jewish here?"

I sighed deeply before responding. "For thousands of years, being Jewish in the world has never been about being comfortable; it's been about living with who you are and loving it."

Carlo contemplated my response and then asked the question that had obviously concerned him since I broke my big news. "And what about this baby?"

"I'd like him to understand all his roots—the Italian ones, the American ones, the Catholic ones, and the Jewish ones."

"Millie, I'm trying hard to understand." Carlo was apparently frustrated. "But this baby would only be one-fourth Jewish. Why cause a problem where it isn't necessary?"

Pow! I had hit the wall. Sometimes, you simply have to accept defeat. Unfortunately, my gut was telling me to drive forward, keep going, keep the pedal to the metal. But that wall was harder than I wanted to admit. How could I marry a man who felt this way? And as I sat in that Italian world with my baby in my belly and my morals so high and mighty, I asked myself, How could I not?

I never answered Carlo's last question. Instead, I gathered my bag and stood up to put my coat back on.

"Are you leaving?" Carlo was incredulous.

"I'm sorry, Carlo, but I don't know how to respond to someone who wants to deny me my right to be who I am." I was crying a little, and I started walking out of the café, secretly praying that Carlo would follow and prove himself to me.

"Wait, Millie!"

He did. Once outside, Carlo pulled me toward him and apologized sincerely. "I didn't mean for it to come out that way. You know English is not my first language." I started to pull away but he insisted. "Millie. Emilia." He sounded like my father resorting to his serious tone. "I love you. Do you love me?" Carlo demanded my answer.

"I thought I did, Carlo, but you're letting me down." I couldn't look at him when I said it.

He pulled me closer. "Look at me."

I obeyed.

"I promise you right now that I will try my very hardest to never let you down again. I want to marry you, and I want our baby to learn whatever you want him to learn." Then Carlo's expression softened and he added, "Perhaps I will learn something too."

CHAPTER 3

▼

In life, there are moments that you will always remember, either because they are so wonderful or because they are so tragic. There are also moments that fall into neither category. They are the ones that cause such trauma that the brain protects itself by tucking those memories so deeply away that, if you are lucky, you will never find them again. I have still not found the words to tell the story of what happened when Carlo announced our engagement. Nor have I been able to recount the conversation that I had with my own parents. My next memories in the chronology of this story are of the marriage ceremony.

Carlo and I were married in a civil ceremony, which really amounted to nothing much in a country whose nuptials are rarely envisioned outside the church. We sat in front of an old wooden desk, which was probably constructed circa 1950, as a middle-aged woman with very strong tobacco breath read aloud the details outlined in the marriage certificate. Her name tag told us that she was Bruna Guarini. As she read, I tried to imagine that I was in the fantasy wedding of my childhood dreams. But no matter how tightly I closed my eyes, I could not turn Bruna into a rabbi, nor could I turn her Italian words into Hebrew chants. I opened my eyes as she asked for our signatures. Carlo signed, and then I signed. A neighboring desk clerk whose name tag read Maria Pia served as our witness. I tried to pretend that it was exotic to have a Maid of Honor named Maria Pia, but the image of Maria Pia's navy sweater vest over her putty-colored, long-sleeved blouse in no way resembled anything that my fantasy Maid of Honor would wear at my fantasy wedding. I thought of my sister, Romy, back home in Florida. At that moment on that gray January day, Romy was surely at the University of Florida, having already returned for her winter semester of her junior year. She was probably in a deep sleep in her sorority house bedroom (as it was 4 o'clock in the morning on the east coast), dreaming of nothing having to do with her older sister's wedding. Romina Gossett should have been my Maid of Honor.

As my new husband and I sat on the steps of the Basilica di San Petronio in Bologna's main square, Piazza Maggiore, I thought of the Church of Santo Stefano. I bet that Carlo would have liked to have gotten married there, in front of his family and friends and with the proud smile that a man deserves to wear when he's reaching one of life's biggest milestones. That's when I realized that Carlo, too, had given up a lot to get married in the way that we had…without any family or love surrounding us.

During the remainder of my pregnancy, Carlo continued living with his mamma while I stayed on in the apartment with Michela. I tried to add more classes to my teaching schedule, but there was nothing else available for me. Carlo, in turn, found a part-time job at a bar near the university. He found himself working so long during the night and studying whenever he wasn't in class that time with me was third priority. The fact that we didn't live together was irrelevant, since we hardly ever saw each other anyway. Even weekends were no guarantee since Carlo wanted to get in as many work hours as he could. As promised, he was trying his hardest not to let me down by earning all that was humanly possible in the short months that were left before the baby would come in early July. Our hopes were to then get our own apartment where we could be a family...without Regina.

Regina Buonsignore had become a widow at the young age of thirty-one. She had a four-year-old son and another child in utero when Enzo Mazzini was killed in an accident on the Autostrada between Bologna and his hometown of Rimini, a resort town on the Adriatic Sea.

Enzo had always loved the shore, but his inland-born wife never shared his passion. For that reason, Enzo often drove alone on the sixty-five-mile journey home to visit family and check up on business. The Mazzini family owned several small hotels which were all managed by either a Mazzini brother or cousin. It was a lucrative industry that seasonally delivered on its economic promise of a good life. Though Enzo loved his family in Bologna, he owed his heart to the tourists of Rimini.

On the tragic night that would change the Mazzini family forever, Enzo enjoyed one too many drinks of *grappa* after a boisterous family dinner with his brothers and their wives. His fate was sealed when he entered the Autostrada in his old Peugeot.

Regina took the news well enough, until she lost the baby the following day. She turned her grief towards her only son, who she affectionately called Carlino, and donned her black mourning clothes for only one week before shelving them and moving on with her life. Regina had never been a passionate woman. She had loved Enzo the way one loves a kind caretaker, giving him his due respect and servicing him when he needed it. For Regina, sex had only served her purpose twice, and now she had changed her count to once since the second baby would never be. Suitors came and suitors went because, as I've already mentioned in so many words, Regina was a bitter pill to swallow. The Buonsignore family was quite financially established in Bologna, and when Enzo Mazzini introduced Regina to widowhood, her economic insecurity caused her to slip down quite a few rungs on the ladder of social climbing. The Rimini Mazzini family had never taken to her and did not feel obligated to include her in a business in which she had never shown interest. Regina's own family offered support, which allowed her to stay in the beautiful apartment on Via Castiglione, but from the age of four, Carlo became her hope for financial and social utopia. Her brilliant boy would grow to earn a very respectable living, marry into another elite Bolognese family, and take care of his mamma so that she could afford the level of luxury in which she had been raised. Then came the Jew, and Regina flinched in shame to imagine Carlo behind the counter of a student bar, serving beer and other spirits to the educationally elite.

Between February and July, I had set a goal for myself, and it was a lofty one; I was going to win over the mamma. On one mid-February afternoon, I found myself alone in La Mela, my favorite little trattoria located in a small piazza at the end of my street. I didn't have a class that day until four o'clock, so I took advantage of my free time to formulate my plan of action. When I thought of all the things I could do right in my mother-in-law's eyes, I realized how daunting a task it was. To prove my point, I let myself remember that first night after Carlo and I got married.

"Isn't *she* supposed to give *us* gifts? We're the ones getting married." As soon as I said the words, I knew my attitude was out of line, and Carlo's silence on the other end of my receiver confirmed that he agreed. "*Va bene.*" All right. I conceded. "I'll stop by the market and pick up some wine before dinner."

On our wedding night, we had been invited to Regina's house for dinner…to celebrate. Carlo had called me on the eve of our wedding to inform me of the invitation. I was to be at his home by 8:30, and he suggested that I bring a bottle of wine as a gift.

"Millie," Carlo's voice had taken on a sweet tone. "Please get the wine from an *enoteca*." A wine seller. "Mamma will know the difference."

The only enoteca I knew was off Via Rizzoli, an out-of-the-way walk from my apartment to Regina's on Via Castiglione. On my first evening as a married woman, I left my apartment early and headed towards Piazza Maggiore…alone. I loved the energy in the streets at this time of the evening when everyone had just gotten off work and was running around, doing their grocery shopping from the fresh market vendors, grabbing a cappuccino with a friend before heading home, or just congregating in the piazza to people-watch.

The piazza was aglow with the city lights of the bordering cafés and Neptune's Fountain, where the Roman god held out his left hand to calm the water below, which streamed from the cisterns of cherubs and the breasts of sirens. The tallest sight in the piazza was the Clock Tower, which rose up majestically behind the Notaries' Palace.

Apart from the architectural wonders of Piazza Maggiore, there were the human ones, and on that night, my two favorite sights had shown themselves. The first was the group of four or five older men who would gather close together in a circular fashion and argue about life. Their dark coats and hats hid their features from view, but the most important element was always visible…the single hand of one man, his thumb firmly pressed against the remaining four fingers as he shook it vehemently in the face of his friend, trying to prove his argument. Many voices would rise and fall as they fought against each other to be heard. My second favorite human attraction was the saxophonist. I never knew his name (I don't know if anyone did), but each night he routinely walked the steps of the basilica playing the same tune over and over…*My Favorite Things*, from The Sound of Music. Though he apparently had an extremely narrow repertoire, I found humor in the off-tempo way that he interpreted the classic tune.

Just off of Piazza Maggiore, I could glimpse down my favorite street, Via delle Pescerie, where fishmongers displayed their fresh catch and shellfish alongside vendors of the fresh fruits and vegetables of the season. It was the most charming and colorful street of the city center, and even if I didn't need to go that way, I always tried to steal a peek as I passed it by.

The night was not as bitterly cold as usual for this time of year, so I was enjoying the breeze against my face as I finished my stroll through the piazza and darted across the busy Via Rizzoli, heading towards an off-street whose name I could never remember but which I recognized by the landmark of the shoe store that I frequented.

Inside the *enoteca*, the mood was quiet, which matched perfectly with the dark walls, the dark floor, and the dark wine bottles stacked like library books on the wall. I had no idea of where to begin, so I enlisted the help of the handsome older gentleman standing behind the bar.

"The thing is," I began in my best Italian. "I just got married."

"Congratulations!" He responded on cue.

"Thank you, but the thing is that my mother-in-law doesn't like me very much, and I'm trying to pick a wine to bring to dinner at her home this evening."

"An Italian mother-in-law?"

I supposed he was asking since it was obvious I was American. "Yes." I rolled my eyes. I couldn't help myself.

"I have the perfect wine for pleasing mammas who are virtually impossible to please." He smiled at me in that way that said, *I've been there, and I feel your pain.*

At 8:45, I stood in the small courtyard leading to Carlo's apartment. I looked at my watch one more time before pressing the button for number 2-A. It had taken all my precise planning and a handful of patience as I intentionally tried *not* to arrive at 8:30. Though it went completely against my grain as a punctual person, I knew that if I showed up at 8:30 exactly, Regina would mock my Americanism and point out that I would never fit in with the Italian culture. The fact of the matter is that fifteen minutes late was still on the early side, but my patience had worn rather thin.

Carlo greeted me in the foyer with a loving kiss and a comforting squeeze. "Everything's going to be all right," he whispered in my ear.

I walked into the dining room to present Regina with my gift. She had set a formal table with her most elegant linens, and for a moment, I felt flattered. From the number of place settings, I could see that others had been invited, and that took me off guard. Regina entered the dining room from the kitchen, and a thin smile spread across her lips upon seeing me.

"*Signora*," I began, trying not to let my voice tremble. "Thank you for inviting me. I've brought some wine for the table." I held the nicely wrapped bottle out for her to accept.

"Emilia, or is it Millie?"

"Millie is fine, *Signora*."

"Millie, did you really think that I could not afford to provide enough wine for my guests?" She stared at me as if she were Torquemada, head of the Spanish Inquisition.

"No, I—" I didn't know what to say. I shot a glance at Carlo, who was back in the foyer greeting a newly-arrived guest. I hadn't even heard the intercom buzzer sound.

Regina's serious expression quickly changed to one of humor. "Relax, girl. I'm kidding." She reached out for the bottle. "Thank you for the thoughtful gift."

I stood in the same spot, frozen, as I watched Regina open the wrapping and survey my selection.

"Carlo," she shouted into the other room. "Did you help her pick this out, or does she have naturally good taste?" She smiled slyly.

Carlo came into the dining room as he responded, "She did it all herself, Mamma."

As they both smiled at me, I felt like a five-year-old who had just learned to tie her shoes for the first time and who should have gratefully appreciated such praise. Then I realized that I was looking at the rest of my life.

Once we were all seated around the table, we were seven people. Regina sat at one head while Uncle Patricio, Regina's brother, sat at the other. On my right sat Carlo, and to my left was Aunt Luciana. Across from us were cousins Paolo and Massimo, both still high school students. Before anyone started eating, Regina finished the final table-setting task of filling the wine glasses. As she approached me, I could see the cunning smile in her eyes. "Would you like a glass of wine, Mille?"

It was a test. She knew I was pregnant, and even though everyone else knew as well, Regina knew the topic was somewhat taboo to discuss. If I refused the glass, it would draw attention to my pregnancy and expose that worst-hidden, dirty little secret. But if I accepted, I would surely be berated for drinking alcohol and not taking care of the baby. Unlike my initial meeting with Regina, I had a bit more confidence now. "No, thank you."

She stood next to me for a moment, the wine bottle tipped and waiting, her close-lipped grin tightly frozen. She seemed to be toying with the idea of how she could mock my response. After what seemed an eternity (I even heard my stomach growl once), she shifted her gaze to Aunt Luciana.

"Certainly *you* will have some wine, Lucia, right?"

"But of course, Regina. What's a toast without wine?"

When the wine had been dispensed, Regina took her rightful place at the head of her table.

"Would you like to make the toast, Regina?" Uncle Patricio lifted his glass in waiting.

Regina did not answer, and for a fleeting moment, I felt pity for her. She was obviously completely uncomfortable with the whole arrangement. What in the world could she possibly say that wouldn't be a lie or that wouldn't incite yelling or, even worse, crying? She was certainly in a pickle, and once I got over my moment of feeling sorry for her, I guiltlessly enjoyed watching her squirm. But then she found her way out. "Patricio, I think it would be more touching if Carlo's favorite uncle made the toast."

Uncle Patricio nodded once in appreciation, and we all lifted our glasses, mine having been filled with water. "To Carlo and Emilia…Health, happiness, and success."

Canned but non-controversial. I liked Uncle Patricio.

As the meal progressed and seconds were inevitably being offered, I knew conflict was in the air. Everyone else had already accepted their heaping next portion while I had no more room to fill my stomach. I had never been a big eater, and I had become even less so since being pregnant and feeling pressure on my stomach sooner than later.

"Millie, would you like more veal?" Regina offered, her large serving fork already spearing a fillet.

"No, thank you." Again, my turn to refuse.

"Luciana, I believe the American doesn't like my cooking?" (At least I was the American instead of the Jew.)

Luciana smiled politely, trying to acknowledge Regina without feeding her fire.

"No, no, *Signora*. It was all wonderful. It's just that I haven't got any more room." I put my hand to my swollen belly.

"Don't you know that you're eating for two now? You can't deprive the baby of food."

It was out there…the baby. And it was time for me to stand my ground. Still, I had to be diplomatic.

"I am sure that the baby has eaten enough this evening. After all, your food was so delicious and nutritious. What more could a baby ask for?" I tried to smile genuinely as I spoke, but Regina wasn't giving up yet.

"Patricio, did you know that Millie is Jewish?"

There it was. My Judaism had trumped my American citizenship at last.

"Really?" Uncle Patricio looked at me inquisitively.

"Yes," responded Regina. "She's even trying to influence Carlino into raising the child Jewish, can you believe it? As if life weren't difficult enough without adding the dirty label of Jew to my grandchild."

She had actually called me a dirty Jew. I put down my fork and looked directly at Carlo as I tried to hold back tears. I was determined not to cry again in Regina's home and not to let that ignorant bitch get the better of me. Fortunately, Carlo rose to the occasion.

"Mamma, I think that is very unnecessary and hurtful. Millie is my wife, and I support her right to be who she is."

What kind of a response was that? I wasn't sure. Before I could give it more thought, Regina had firmly put down her wine glass and was glaring at Carlo.

"You will support your family, who has supported you your whole life!"

Be strong, Carlo, I prayed.

"I am soon going to have my own family to support. I will support everyone who I love, Mamma."

Now, I really had no idea of what had happened. Had my husband defended me, or had he given the most ambiguous yet cryptic response that he could come up with under pressure? I felt nauseated. It wasn't necessary to look around the table to sense the thick wall of tension encircling all of us. The cousins had already finished everything on their plates, opting for the shovel-in-the-food-and-shut-out-the-conversation mode of survival. Aunt Luciana excused herself to go to the bathroom, and Uncle Patricio just sat in his seat, staring down at his food as he rubbed his temples with both hands. Finally, Regina spoke. "For God's sake! I didn't mean to start a war here. Can we please enjoy the rest of our dinner?"

Could it be that simple? Did Regina hate me just because I was Jewish? My own innocence would not allow me to accept that at face value. There had to be more to it, but now wasn't the time to ponder such deep thoughts. I followed my hostess's orders and returned to my plate, moving the remaining crumbs around with my fork in order to feign eating.

The rest of the evening was less eventful as *grappa* and *limoncello* made their way to the table as the traditional after-dinner drinks. The family chatted about various topics, including the economy, the laziness of southerners, and if Berlusconi should have remained in office as Prime Minister. As more alcohol flowed, so did the laughter until I actually believed that Regina was happy. Alcohol has a way of softening people on the one hand and bringing out their true feelings on the other. And when the cousins had already gone home and it was time for me to say goodnight, Regina left me with words that confused and frightened me at the same time. "Take care of yourself, Emilia. We wouldn't want anything to happen to that baby of yours."

It was the first Friday in February, and I had just had an ultrasound. I was eighteen weeks pregnant, and my baby was apparently in good condition and growing quite well. I held in my left hand the photograph of the ultrasound, which revealed my child in profile, his small spine resembling a string of pearls. One hand was suspended above his belly; it looked like he was waving at me. During the procedure, the technician had asked me if I wanted to know the sex. Since coming to Italy, there had already been too many unexpected happenings in my life. I decided that I did not need any more surprises; I wanted to have some knowledge of the future. That is how I found out that my baby was a boy.

I left the obstetrician's office at seven o'clock and headed right for the bar where Carlo worked. He would be on his shift all night, but it would be calm enough at this hour to catch a few words with him and show him the picture. When I opened the entrance door, I could see Carlo drying some glasses behind the counter. As always, he was so handsome…the kind of bartender that any girl would want to flirt with. That thought had often made me uncomfortable, so I immediately threw it on my back burner and approached him with my head held high and my belly a bit more protruding than I would have chosen.

"Hi, handsome!" I approached him with my flirtiest voice.

He smiled back in that way he had of completely disarming me with one wide grin.

"Would you like to see the most handsome little boy in the world?" I waved the ultrasound photo in the air in a teasing manner, but Carlo's face had lost all its rich color.

"You know the sex? You're telling me the sex?"

They weren't questions as much as blatant statements of incredulity. I froze in my place, letting the flimsy photo paper hang from my fingers like a dead leaf. I didn't dare speak a word.

"Millie," Carlo was shaking his head in disbelief. "Isn't it enough that our life is less than idyllic, that our wedding was a particularly lonely affair, and that our baby is being received into this world with far less enthusiasm than a child deserves? Why do you have to ruin a potentially exciting moment by knowing it all?" He paused and waited for me to respond, but I still said nothing. Then he screamed, "You don't know it all! In fact, you don't know anything, Millie!"

I flinched. Then I turned on my heels and ran out of the bar into the welcoming energy of the city streets. I didn't know where to go. I felt completely deflated and mildly confused. Had I missed some cultural clues? How was I supposed to know that finding out the sex of your baby was such a destructive piece of information? It had been a while since I had felt so helpless, and I thought that nothing anyone could say to me could make me feel smaller at that moment.

Suddenly, I had a change of heart and I felt courageous. It was as if I had reached my very bottom and had no where to go but up. I could handle anyone at that moment, so I decided to do just that. I headed up Via Castiglione towards Regina's apartment, focusing on my goal of winning over the mamma.

She greeted me with a hesitant smile, obviously surprised to see me and taken off guard by my sense of self-possession. We walked into the salon before either of us said anything. "To what do I owe the pleasure of your visit, Emilia?" She sat down in an easy chair and motioned for me to take a seat on the sofa, but I didn't sit. Instead, I held out the ultrasound photo with a shy smile.

"I wanted to share this with you."

Regina slowly rose from the comfort of her chair and reached for the photo. It took all my will not to say a word and just let her take it in. There wasn't anything she could say that could hurt me more than Carlo's words had; I was sure of it. I waited patiently as Regina studied the picture, praying that she would have as difficult a time as

I had in identifying the ultrasound image of male genitals. A moment passed before I saw her expression soften into one previously unrecognizable to me.

"This is Carlos's baby." Her eyes never left the photo.

"Yes, it is." I chose my pronoun very carefully as I assured her in my softest voice, trying not to ruin the sanctity of our brief moment of connection. Regina looked up at me and said nothing more for what seemed an eternity. Then, she turned toward the kitchen and motioned for me to follow.

"Come! Let's have some coffee."

People are funny birds. The proof lies in that odd expression, invented not by birds but by people. *He's a funny bird. She's a strange bird.* What does it mean? It means that people are strange and unpredictable such that there are times when you don't even know if you're dealing with a person, a bird, or some other undiscovered life form. In Regina's case, I had thought that she was an open book, but she went right ahead and proved me wrong. What a funny bird. Looking back now, it seems to me that when Carlo knocked me down so low, I was able to find that hidden bravado that I had so longed to have. And when faced with such a funny bird, Regina had no choice but to deal with me as someone other than the weak, trouble-making, Jewish daughter-in-law.

I recently read on the Internet an article titled, *Rules for Being Human*, from Cherie Carter-Scott in her book, *Chicken Soup for the Soul*. Rule number seven says, "Others are merely mirrors of you. You cannot love or hate something about another person unless it reflects something you love or hate about yourself." I asked myself what it was that I hated about Regina and how that could possibly reflect my own weaknesses. It was her overbearing and condescending nature that I resented. I knew I hated her for that because I had often let others control me or talk down to me, and I hated myself for being so easily manipulated. Then I asked myself why Regina hated me and what it could reflect in her personal mirror of self-reflection, but all I could do was imagine because I wasn't Regina. I imagined that she resented me for being the recipient of Carlos's love, which would ultimately mean that she would no longer be. I imagined that she resented me for being at that starting point in my life where the future of my family was in my hands...a future of which she had been robbed when Enzo Mazzini died on an Italian highway. Or maybe it was just because I was Jewish. It was all conjecture; I would never really know. But that day in Regina's kitchen, sitting around the small wooden table for two, Carlo's mamma and Carlo's baby's mamma enjoyed a friendly chat over two hot cups of coffee.

We chatted about many things. I learned the story of Carlo's birth and at what ages he accomplished almost all of his baby milestones. He sat at five months, crawled at seven months, and walked on his first birthday to perfectly commemorate the occasion. I learned about Carlo's childhood and the playful times he had with his cousins from Rimini. (It was the first time I had ever heard mention of Rimini either from Carlo or Regina.) I even saw photographs of Carlo at various school ages.

Our visit lasted about two hours before I realized how tired I was and thanked Regina sincerely for the coffee and, more importantly, the stories. As I walked home on that chilly evening, I felt happier than I'd felt in a long time. I had actually fooled myself into believing that I'd won over the mamma.

Carlo's outburst in the bar was soon forgotten when he heard my rendition of coffee talk with his mamma. At first, he couldn't quite believe my story until his mother corroborated it. I didn't mind his doubt since I, myself, would not have believed it if I hadn't been there. Carlo was summarily pleased with my coup and my good judgment in not sharing my knowledge of the baby's gender with Mamma, and so the next few months in Bologna went as smoothly as a couple could hope for.

At this point, I must step back and force myself to remember that all was not as smooth in Miami as it was in Bologna, as should be expected. After all, I had crossed an ocean, conceived a child out of wedlock, and then married a foreign man without any family as witness. And I did all this without consulting my parents. You will recall that Allan and Karen had once lived in my new hometown of Bologna and had also conceived a child there. The primary difference would be that they were already married to each other when said baby came into the picture, and they had returned to the States before said baby was born, allowing other loved ones to share in the joy of their new family. Had they known that twenty-two years later said child would telephone them one day from thousands of miles away and report that she was pregnant and had just wed the baby's father, Allan and Karen might have actually considered giving said child up for adoption in order to avoid such unspeakable deception and heartbreak. This may sound dramatic, but my parents were dramatic people. I had telephoned them once in January after the wedding and once again around April to report that I was doing well and thinking of them. They had never picked up the phone themselves to check in on me, nor had they asked if I'd be returning to Miami. It was as if I'd been lost, and they were quickly on their road to acceptance. Grieving was not their style.

Let me attempt to justify my behavior by saying that an ocean is very powerful. The United States is vast yet so well connected that two relatives or close friends can live in Miami and Los Angeles and still feel very much in touch. They can affordably hop a plane from one coast to the other and chat by phone for free if they find the right calling plan. With 3,000 miles and three time zones between them, the Floridian and the Californian can still feel like they are virtually next door to each other. But the Atlantic Ocean is a formidable body of water. Although the distance between the east coast of the United States and the western-most coast of Europe is shorter than the width of the U.S. mainland, its implications are much stronger. On either side of the Atlantic Ocean, things look quite different. The scenery, the climate, the smells, the languages, the architecture, the people, and even the color of the sky remind American tourists that they are a world away from their own land. With that physical change come the psychological changes in attitude and behavior for one living in a foreign land, and when I first arrived in Italy (an ocean and three countries away from Miami), I fell into that mindset. I believed that my actions in Italy would have no bearing on my life in the States. It was like that commercial for Las Vegas, which I would see twelve years later, that said, *What happens here stays here.* I felt protected by the ocean as if it were some impenetrable barrier that would let me be who I wanted to be in Bologna and not affect who I used to be in Miami. On some level, I think I even floated through my pregnancy half-believing that it wasn't really happening at all and that whenever I wanted to return to Miami, there would be no baby. In hindsight, I believe that my lack of contact with my parents was a subconscious decision to protect my messed up fantasy life in Bologna so that I'd be able to someday return to Miami untarnished. It may sound strange or, even worse, delirious, but I never missed my parents or my sister while I was in Bologna. I went through my days as Carlo's pregnant wife, patiently awaiting the arrival of our son and the time when we would be able to live together as a family.

As July approached and the academic term came to a close, my roommate Michela made life easier for Carlo and me. She announced that she would be returning to Ravenna for the summer and then moving in with her boyfriend when she returned for her

Fall classes in October. Carlo and I could assume her half of the lease, and we would convert Michela's bedroom into a nursery.

On July 1, 1995, as I lazily watched Michela pack up her belongings, I went into labor. Eight hours later and one day before my twenty-third birthday, my son was born in the presence of my doctor, my husband, and God. Choosing his name was easy. Jewish people traditionally name their children for family members who have passed away, and Carlo wanted to honor his father's memory. That is how the second Enzo Mazzini came to be.

On July second, I awoke in the hospital to find a colorful banner spread over my bed sheets. The previous night, Carlo had been sent home to sleep but instead had labored through his own exhaustion to make me a special birthday surprise. It read, *Congratulations and Happy Birthday to Enzo's Mamma!*

As I read the banner again and again, it hit me; I was now the mamma. For better or for worse, I now had the unalienable right to love my son and be respected as the mamma. I was Enzo's mamma…forever.

In my first days and weeks with Enzo, I would study his features, his body, his unique proportion. I felt the need to know my child inside and out as if my time with him were limited. It was a terrible feeling—almost premonition-like, but instead of voicing my fears, I chalked it up to baby blues and all the fears and anxiety that can accompany postpartum depression.

The truth is that I never really felt depressed. I never had negative thoughts towards Enzo, Carlo, or myself, and I never broke into tears for no apparent reason. I simply felt that my time with my son was precious and meant to be brief. I secretly expected to receive bad news every time I took Enzo to the pediatrician. I expected some rare childhood disease or syndrome to be diagnosed, confirming my anxiety about fleeting time. I avoided seeing my own doctor for fear of receiving my own fateful diagnosis. Instead, I took count-less photographs both with my camera and my mind's eye, and I felt a mild sense of panic each time I lost sight of my child, though such an occurrence was very rare since I was Enzo's sole caregiver.

Carlo had begun his final year of study and was continuing to work at the bar, while Regina would only offer help if I left Enzo at her house. I was rarely willing to do that and therefore had very little time to myself. Still, I didn't mind. As I said before, I sensed that my motherhood phase of life was not meant to be long-lived. I never told anyone about my fears for two reasons: there was no one around to listen, and even if there had been, I was sure they would think I was insane.

"I would like to have Enzo baptized soon. When do you think would be a good time?"

Carlo and I were sitting at the table having lunch together…a rare happening in the Mazzini household. On this particular day, I had been forewarned that he would be making the time to come home between classes, so I had prepared a full lunch. Enzo was rest-lessly napping in his crib as Carlo and I were just beginning our first dish of a three-course meal.

Enzo was four months old, and Carlo and I had been married for almost ten months. If the fly on the wall could talk, he would have thought he was observing a couple married for far too long with very little left to discuss. That's how I felt about Carlo as well. Though our common language had converted from English to Ital-ian over time, it made no difference. We rarely talked anyway, so no matter the language, our communication was minimal. We simply worked together as a team when necessary, which was mostly during the middle of the night. Enzo was still not a sleep-through-the-night baby. Therefore, Carlo and I were not the well-rested parents who should have been enjoying the honeymoon stage associated with the first year of marriage. It was a strange life I led in those times, and Carlo's question over lunch was to be the beginning of even stranger days.

Baptism? I pondered the question before answering too hastily. I decided to take an unorthodox approach. "Do you know what I really appreciated about you, Carlo?"

"What?" He shoveled a spoonful of tortellini soup into his mouth without looking at me.

"When Enzo and I were still in the hospital and you allowed me to have him circumcised."

Carlo finally looked up. "Why was that a big deal? I'm circumcised."

"Yes," I conceded, "But I knew that you didn't want Enzo to have a formal *bris* when he was eight days old. So I appreciated it when you didn't give me a hassle about having it done in the hospital."

Carlo apparently didn't know where I was going with this. "Well, you're welcome, I guess."

"All I'm saying, Carlo, is that I gave up one of my Jewish traditions without much fight, but that didn't mean that I was willing to baptize our son."

"Why not?" Carlo had almost finished his soup, while mine remained untouched.

"Because if he couldn't be officially Jewish by having his *bris*, then he can't be officially Catholic by having a baptism. Fair is fair."

There was a long silence that I decided to interpret as agreement, and I finally let myself enjoy the now cold soup in front of me. The apartment was very quiet except for the sounds of soup spoons against bowls and the occasional whimper from Enzo in the next room. Many couples like to talk about the comfortable silence that they can share together, but this was in no way comforting. I finished my soup quickly and rose to collect Carlo's bowl and mine before serving the second course. I put the two bowls gently in the sink, trying not to make too much clamor. In the quiet stillness of the apartment, such noises seemed to echo in their deep desire to break the tension. I carefully dished out the chicken scaloppini with asparagus onto two plates and tried to place them down gingerly. Still, the sound of Carlo's plate hitting the wooden table was louder than I'd expected, and I actually jumped a bit. Before I could sit down to enjoy my own plate, Carlo broke the silence. "Mamma has already booked the church for next month."

Still standing with my own plate in one hand, I turned toward our bedroom and walked away from Carlo.

"Millie!" He shouted. "Come back and eat with me. We need to talk about this."

I closed the bedroom door and sat at the foot of the bed with my plate of chicken on my lap. I allowed myself to eat the entire serving before expending any emotional energy on the issue. When I heard Enzo's cry as he awoke from his nap, I didn't budge. I waited patiently to see if Carlo would rise to the occasion and attend to his son. I heard Carlo shower our baby with Italian terms of endearment, and Enzo's cries soon subsided. If Carlo couldn't win me over, he was going to try his damned hardest with Enzo.

Back in our bedroom, I placed my empty plate on the nightstand and then curled up in bed. Every fiber of my being told me that this marriage could only lead to no good and that I should get out fast. But in the real world in which we all live, we are taught almost from day one to ignore our instincts and better judgment. We are taught not to jump to conclusions and to think rationally instead of impulsively. The logical person is more respected than the emotional one, who is seen as immature and oftentimes unstable.

As children, we are allowed to foster dreams about our future, no matter how fantastical they sound, but such ideas are only tolerated up to a certain point. At around the same time when we're supposed to stop believing in Santa Claus or the Tooth Fairy, we're also expected to understand that princesses don't always live happily ever after and neither do most mommies and daddies. The conflict of cultural pressure and the desire to believe in dreams is a strong one, and it isn't really until deep into adolescence that we can really grasp the idea of how hard life can be. Even then, truth be told, privileged teenagers have no earthly idea of what hard means because they're far from finished growing up. They go to college and pretend to be adults playing with adult relationships. They pretend to be on the road to educational and professional accomplishment, but they are really just large children hanging on to secret fantasies about the perfect job and the perfect relationship. Then comes graduation and the real world, followed by an awkward time when they're too old to hang out with the college crowd but too young to be taken seriously by society. That's the stage I was in when I transversed the Atlantic Ocean, started working in Italy, fell in love, found myself pregnant, got married, and became a mother. And I still harbored dreams of my picturesque family with my handsome husband and my perfect baby.

I got out of bed and walked to the mirror, which was mounted on the armoire door. I stared at my twenty-three-year-old face. My dark brown eyes and fair skin appeared more in contrast than usual, and my long, wavy, honey-colored locks looked particularly dull. There had been moments when I would see myself and think that I still looked sixteen. But more recently, there were moments when I thought I looked thirty. Ironic, I thought, that I was exactly between those two ages. It seemed that my soul did not quite know which age to reflect. Then my reflection spoke to me. I watched my lips move, but I didn't feel myself making the sounds. So I just listened.

"You have messed up your life," the face in the mirror said. "Here is the truth, so listen carefully. If you had never gotten pregnant, Carlo would be nothing more than another name from your past, another nostalgic love affair to remember, another face whose beautiful features would have already disappeared from your memory."

I nodded in agreement and secretly asked myself how my life would be different if I had terminated my pregnancy.

"But if you had not kept your baby," my reflection continued, seeming to read my mind, "You would be roaming Bologna right now, involving yourself in another stupidly romantic passion, potentially making the same mistake over and over with the same guy under a different name."

So what do I do now?

"Your son came into this world to teach you something. You just need to figure out what it is that you're supposed to be learning. Carlo is not going to teach you this lesson; that is Enzo's job."

There was a soft knock on the bedroom door. "Mille? Are you all right? Who are you talking to?"

I didn't answer but instead maintained my gaze with the mirror. I repeated to myself, "That is Enzo's job."

CHAPTER 4

▼

Dreams and nightmares; the latter usually speak of fear, confusion, and even terror, while the former tend to represent the opposing emotions of hope, clarity and fantasy. But what of dreams that seem never-ending…the kind from which you cannot awake? What about the dreams whose images are so real to the brain that, even if you can force yourself to awake, the body can't immediately recover and resume the status quo? Are those dreams good? Do they actually offer a sense of hope, clarity and fulfilled fantasies? Or are they like a drug, forcing your mind to ignore outside stimuli and only obey the impulses coming from within?

Sometimes life is like a drugged dream. In the days following the announcement of my son's impending baptism, I felt out of control. When I slept, my dreaming experiences felt more real than my waking sensations. With my eyes opened, I saw the world around me, but I felt as if I were watching my life going on from some distant point outside of my body. I saw myself feeding Enzo his bottle, changing his diaper, bathing him, playing with him, singing songs to him, and holding him in my arms.

Enzo's eyes were golden hazel like his father's but almond-shaped like mine. His soft skin was the color of cappuccino like his father's, but his full head of curly hair was the same honey color as mine. And his mouth was all Gossett with a rosy-lipped smile that almost spread from ear to ear. If my parents could see him, they would certainly say that he reminded them of me as a baby but with lighter eyes and toastier skin. My parents...the thought of them was too painful, so I pushed it away and kissed Enzo's forehead, letting his natural body heat warm my lonely lips.

Throughout my period of self-separation (which is how I've come to name that time in my life), there was one belief from which I never wavered. I knew that I loved my son and that he would always be my son, no matter which house of God claimed him as its own.

I chose not to fight the baptism, mostly because I preferred my self-inflicted exile from Carlo and Regina and felt too tired to prepare an adequate defense. I stood in the church and watched Uncle Patricio and Aunt Luciana assume the roles of godparents. Enzo slept peacefully in Aunt Luciana's arms until the priest dripped the tepid holy water over his forehead and soaked his shiny curls, causing him to wake from his baby dreams and cry out in utter disapproval. I closed my eyes tightly and let Enzo's cries fill me up, pretending that they were my own stifled screams of rebellion. At the moment of Enzo's baptism, he became free of his original sin. I, on the other hand, was moving further and further away from my own salvation.

When the ceremony was over and everyone was making their way up the aisle, I suddenly felt someone grab my upper arm. Regina had caught up with me and had taken a firm hold before whispering in my ear. Even after she had backed off and fallen in with the others, her words rang through my head as loud as church bells. "This child will not be Jewish."

Back in Regina's apartment, I watched a small group of family and friends mingle and pick at food platters that Regina had prepared. I had turned myself into a wallflower in order to escape the chit-chat and to indulge my deceptive thoughts. I imagined what it would take for me to leave Italy and take Enzo with me. First, I would have to get Enzo naturalized so he could have an American passport. Then I would need to contact my parents and convince them to lend me money for the overseas air fare. I knew they would do it, but the thought of initiating contact under such circumstances was terrifying. Instead of dwelling on that step, I jumped back to the first and formulated the plan in my mind. Monday morning, I would pack up Enzo's diaper bag for a day trip and catch the train to Florence, where the closest American consulate would surely be the place to get the ball rolling. (Mental note to self: don't forget passport.) While in Florence, I would try to do a bit of sightseeing, if the consulate didn't hold me up all day and in case my departure from Italy happened sooner than later. No matter what, I had to be home before six o'clock, when Carlo usually returned from the university for a little break before running off to the bar to work. Counting the approximate ninety-minute train ride between Bologna and Florence, I would have to run a very tight ship to accomplish all my plans.

Satisfied with my organizational skills, I relaxed and realized that I needed to use the restroom. I headed down the small hallway that led to the bathroom but stopped when I recognized Regina and Carlo's voices talking in hushed tones.

"Well, Carlo, you decided to marry the girl, so now you've got yourself a problem."

Everyone else was in the salon, so I held my bladder and gave in to my temptation to eavesdrop.

"Aren't you proud to have a grandson, Mamma?"

"Of course!" exclaimed Regina. "But now we're attached to the child, and I don't trust that Jew as far as I can throw her."

"It has nothing to do with her being Jewish, Mamma." Carlo argued meekly.

"She's got that look in her eye, Carlo, like a deer caught in the headlights. She could run at any moment and take that beautiful baby with her."

"You really think she would do that?"

I found Carlo's innocence charming, but not so Regina. She cursed a few times and finished Carlo off with a stinging insult.

"You and your father...both fools who let people manipulate you!"

I had to admit that Regina was right. Carlo was a fool, but Regina was the bigger fool for not seeing how she had created that characteristic in her own son. At times, I thought to myself that Regina's power of manipulation could rival that of Hitler, but then I would curse myself for having such hateful thoughts about Carlo's mamma. I was often torn between my innate sense of respect for others and my desire to respect myself. It seemed that in the case of my mother-in-law, unfortunately, the two could not co-exist.

Monday morning arrived bringing the typical gray December skies and the light, early winter drizzle that made traveling with an infant absolutely no fun at all. While Carlo had been out working the night before, I had packed my bag for the day, but I still had fresh baby bottles to organize.

I quietly got out of bed and turned to look at my husband sleeping peacefully. Although I still found him incredibly handsome, I felt no attraction towards him. I realized that I didn't really know him well and that I didn't care to learn any more about him than I believed I already knew. I stood by the bed for a long moment, feeling rather callous and angry. Then I forced myself to take the first steps toward the kitchen and leave my anger behind because I knew that Carlo was not to blame. I had made my own choices, and although I had felt helpless at the time of decision-making, I'd still been the one to make my choices. My mother had once told me that, barring being held at gunpoint, absolutely nobody could make me do anything that I didn't want to do. She said that as long as I remembered that, I would never need to waste my energy blaming others for my actions. As I measured out several bottles and padded my bag with ice packs, I knew that she was right. I knew that it was time for me to take responsibility for my life and my son's, even if it meant separating him from his father. It wasn't that Carlo was a bad man; on the contrary, he was a good man with a weak character and an overbearing mother who would live forever, if she had anything to say about it. I believed that the chances of Carlo developing a backbone to stand up to his mother were as remote as Enzo's chances of learning religious tolerance if he grew up under the strong arm of Regina.

By 9:30 that morning, Carlo was at the university while Enzo and I waited patiently on our platform for the intercity train to Florence. By 11:15, I was standing outside the train station in Florence with Enzo strapped securely in my baby harness, the diaper bag slung over my left shoulder, and a map of the city clenched in my right hand as I tried to figure out where the consulate was located. By 11:30, we had reached the American consulate, thanks to the help of a very kind taxi driver. By one o'clock in the afternoon, I was exhausted. I had taken a number upon my arrival and had been doing everything possible to entertain Enzo while maintaining my sanity during a wait that had almost outlasted my train ride. And then my number was up.

A surly, older gentleman with a marked Minnesota accent greeted me with tired eyes and a brusque manner.

"Passport?" He tapped the metal tray between us, motioning for me to slide my passport under the glass partition.

"Yes, hello," I started.

"Passport." He repeated without making eye contact.

I obeyed and slid my passport into his reach. "I would like an application for naturalization for my son, please."

"He's already a U.S. citizen," the man said. "You need the application for a Consular Report of Birth Abroad." He slid the appropriate form under the partition and continued. "This form must be filled out by both parents and returned with payment of 15,000 lire, payable by cash or money order only. Personal check or credit card is not accepted." He spoke like an old recording that had been played too many times, his voice scratchy from wear and tear, but I wasn't listening anymore. I had lost him at, *This form must be filled out by both parents.* How was I going to pull this off without Carlo's participation? "You'll also need supporting documents, which include both parents' birth certificates, marriage certificate, passports, and the child's own birth certificate."

Again, my heart sunk low. I had no idea how long it would take me to get hold of my own birth certificate, let alone Carlo's. Then I had a question. "My husband is Italian. Do you need his passport too?"

"That's what I said," the clerk almost grunted.

"Why?" I was very frustrated.

"Pursuant to Italian law, your child is also a citizen of Italy. And even if he holds another citizenship, his Italian citizenship prevails over all others. He cannot travel across Italian borders without the Italian passport, even to reside in a foreign country. But since he is under five years of age and does not hold a U.S. passport, he can only appear on his father's Italian passport and can only travel with him."

I was almost in tears and tried to appeal to the clerk's human side, which I hoped existed. "Sir, what do I do if my husband is not available to fill out the application or present his passport? I mean, he works so hard and he—"

"Not available?" The clerk cut me off, making eye contact for the first time during our conversation. His look was undoubtedly condescending.

"Not willing," I corrected myself.

"Then I'd say you've got your work cut out for you." He grinned subtly. "These rules are in effect, Ma'am, to protect the children and prevent kidnappings and the sort." The clerk looked down his nose at me, practically accusing me of contemplating kidnapping and confirming that his human side had probably been left behind years ago in Minnesota. Then, suddenly, he seemed to soften. He sighed deeply before he spoke. "Okay, lady. I'm gonna give you some helpful information right now, so listen up. Your work permit expired last June, and it appears that you haven't left Italy since before that time. Am I right?"

I was unaware that I had let my legal status lapse, so I had to come up with a good answer quickly. "I thought my husband had taken care of things when we got married last January."

"Well, there's nothing on record here. No permanent residency application. No request to extend your stay. So here's what you're going to do. Without your baby," he paused and looked at Enzo for the first time. "You will cross the Italian border as quickly as possible and return as a tourist. Then you'll be here legally for six months, giving you plenty of time to take care of things."

"And if I can't get away so soon? It's the Christmas season." I was fearful, but the clerk had lost patience with me.

"I suggest you get busy and stay out of legal trouble in the meantime. Anymore questions?"

I had not a one. "No, thank you." I gathered my bag and held Enzo closer to me as I turned my back on the Minnesotan and exited the consulate, leaving behind the security of American soil. It was lunchtime, but I had lost my appetite as well as my desire to tour Florence.

Enzo and I returned to Bologna by 3:30 in the afternoon. He had napped during the entire train ride and was therefore wide awake as I pushed his stroller into Piazza Maggiore. Instead of continuing on home, I grabbed a quick coffee from one of the many bars lining the piazza and parked the stroller near the steps of San Petronio. Enzo liked being outside and loved people-watching; it made him laugh out loud. He especially loved the piazza's iconic saxophone player, who just happened to be out on that chilly afternoon, hugging his sax and playing on and on about his favorite things.

These are a few of my favorite things: Enzo's staccato giggle and his gold-flecked eyes; a perfect bowl of *tagliatelli al ragu*; the smell of garlic wafting through the streets of the fresh market; my memories of the first day I met Carlo; and sharing a deep belly laugh with my sister, Romy.

What would Romy have to say if she could see me today? She had been the only family member with whom I maintained any semblance of contact. Still, we rarely spoke on the phone, mostly because I could never coordinate a good time to find her and because she was so good at writing me letters, to which I rarely responded. I had certainly made some big mistakes by cutting my family off at this time of my life, and as I sat on the church's steps, I knew that a telephone reunion was imminent. But what would I say to my folks? Where would I begin?

As I thought about the consulate clerk's observation of my visa status, I cursed out loud. How could I have been so careless? When my teaching contract had ended in June, I was one month shy of giving birth and had no plans to return to work so soon, but I had forgotten to leave the country. I knew the laws, so how could I have not followed up with Carlo to secure my legal status in his country, especially before our son was born? I looked at Enzo, who was watching several pigeons congregate around the base of his stroller.

They were hoping to catch some of the crumbs from the crackers that I had placed on the stroller tray. I felt like an incompetent mother, and I started to cry silently. I let the tears roll down my face without wiping them away. I liked how the cold air on my wet face stung badly and how the people nearby noticed me and then quickly averted their glances. It was like punishment for my sins. I imagined myself wearing a scarlet "I" for Irresponsible Mother.

I decided that I had to talk to Carlo.

Two nights before Christmas Eve, Carlo was given the night off and told that he would be working the holiday shift. He informed me that we could have dinner together if I wanted to cook something nice. I bought the finest veal cutlets and the freshest vegetables that I could find to prepare one of Carlo's favorite dishes. I wanted to make this dinner so pleasant that he would be amenable to just about anything. I was even prepared to seduce him if necessary, which would really take him by surprise since it had been many months since we had shared any level of intimacy.

When he came home, I had the table set and two glasses of Chianti ready and waiting. I greeted him with a soft kiss on the mouth and handed him his glass of wine. He looked surprised, pleased, and uncomfortable at the same time. Enzo was on the salon floor, playing on his play mat, and he smiled broadly when he saw his daddy walk into the room. Carlo took one sip of wine, put down the glass, and went to hug his son. The whole scene, from the aroma of the spices on the cooking veal to the relaxed look in Carlo's eyes as he held his son, was enough to make me doubt my ulterior motives. I quickly finished my first glass of wine, seeking the strength and bravado that I would need to not cop out. I poured myself a second glass, and our dinner began.

Small talk, small talk, and more small talk. Finally, I braved the waters. "I've been thinking about my family back in Miami lately."

"Really?" Carlo's interest was piqued.

"Yes. In fact, I've been thinking of calling my parents and possibly visiting them. I'd like to take Enzo with me so they can meet him."

"Wow," Carlo looked up at me. "Wouldn't it be more affordable to have them come here to visit you?"

"Sure, but I'd have to have a lot of nerve to initiate contact and then tell them to cross the ocean to come see me. I think I owe them something for having cut them off for so long, don't you?"

"Where will we find the money?"

"I don't really know right now, but there's a more important issue. If you agree that Enzo can come with me, then we need to get him an American passport." I steeled myself for Carlo's reaction.

"What's wrong with an Italian passport?"

"Well, I've done a bit of research." I stopped when Carlo looked up at me again, this time with concern in his eyes. "And he can't leave the country without you unless he has a U.S. passport."

"Millie?" Carlo swallowed the bit of food in his mouth and looked me squarely in the eyes. "Are you thinking of taking our son back to the States and staying there?" My husband was surely direct, and his bluntness took me off guard.

"No, Carlo!" I lied. "What makes you think such a thing?"

"Mamma said you had that look in your eye, like you could run away at any given moment."

I was too startled to say anything, so I hoped my silence would protect me instead of digging me into a deeper ditch. Carlo didn't speak either. He returned to his meal and avoided my frightened gaze. Finally, I spoke, but my voice was barely audible. "I just want my parents to know their grandson."

Carlo never looked up but responded, "Then tell them to come to Italy."

For the time being, I had lost the passport battle, so I picked another mode of attack. "All right then. I have a different bone to pick with you."

"Feeling bold tonight, are we?" Carlo's sarcasm fueled my fire.

"The thing is, Carlo, we've been married for almost one year, but you've done nothing to start the process of my permanent residency. It almost looks like you don't want me to stay in Italy."

Carlo had the expression of one who has been accused of a crime. "*I* am the one who was supposed to apply for *your* permanent residency?"

"Yes. I am the foreigner. I have no idea of what has to be done. And now my work permit has expired, and I'm actually here illegally. Are you aware of that?" I hoped that playing dumb would work in my favor.

"So, what? They can deport you?" He looked mildly concerned.

"Maybe. And then who would take care of Enzo?" I was working on scare tactics at this point.

"Mamma."

We both froze. The ease with which Carlo provided an answer and called my bluff shocked us both, but I wasn't going down so quickly. I slammed down my water glass and stood up. "You'd better ask for the day off tomorrow before Christmas comes because you're on baby duty." I was almost shouting. "I'm taking the morning train into Switzerland, getting my passport stamped at the border, catching the next train back into Italy, and coming home faster than you can say Regina Buonsignore!"

I scooped Enzo up into my arms and stormed into the nursery, slamming the bedroom door behind me. I sat down in the baby rocker and hugged my son tightly. My breathing was heavy and my heart was racing, but I felt empowered. I had finally stood up for myself and for my son.

It took me almost three hours on the train to arrive in Lugano, Switzerland on December 23, 1995. My first task in the train station was to find passport control and make sure to get stamped. In reality, it wasn't always a guarantee that passports were stamped, and at times, you actually had to request it. By eleven o'clock in the morning, I was officially out of Italy and free to return as an American tourist. I checked the train schedules and found that my first returning journey would depart in forty-five minutes. I perused the timetables to see that such a hurried return was not necessarily my only option. If I was willing to hang out in Lugano for about five hours, I could return later and be back in Bologna by seven o'clock that evening. Sure, the considerate thing to do would be to rush back home and take Enzo off of Carlo's hands, but I wasn't feeling so considerate at that moment. I poked my head out the station entry doors and stole a peek at Lugano. Without doubt, it merited more than just a passport stamp. I walked over to the ticket counter, purchased my return ticket, and headed out into Lugano, Switzerland to find myself some Swiss cheese and Lindt chocolate.

Though I spent what amounted to no more than half a day in that Italian Swiss town, Lugano was one of those places that stay with you forever. When I left the train station, I took the ten-minute walk into the city center, making my way to the spacious Piazza della Riforma. It was a huge square lined with cafés— an even better people-watching locale than Piazza Maggiore. After having the requisite cappuccino in the piazza, I headed behind the Civic Palace to find the picturesque Lake Lugano.

All those fairy tale images that I had harbored for twenty-three years had suddenly come to life, but my imagination hadn't done them justice. Lake Lugano was nothing short of Heaven on Earth. Because it was wintertime in Switzerland when I had the pleasure of visiting, I had bundled myself so completely that only my eyes and nose were exposed to the elements. When I set my numb eyelids upon the splendor of Lake Lugano, I felt a serenity overcome me. I turned my face up to the bluest sky I had ever seen and unwrapped my wool scarf from around my neck. I pulled my cap off of my head and let the winter breeze touch every inch of my face. The smell and the taste of the air mixed with the sound of life moving across the lake filled me in a way I hadn't anticipated. I breathed in deeply, and the frigid air burned my lungs. It forced me to cough, and I had to exhale quickly many times to warm up my insides. Strange as it may sound, the shock was stimulating. After a few minutes, I was compelled to cover up once more as the blood flow to my face slowed down and I felt my nose and lips going numb. I thanked God for touching me and started the southern walk along the lake, eventually winding up a small street that met with Via Nassa, a shopping haven for those into international designer labels.

Eventually, Via Nassa led me to the Church of St. Mary of the Angels. In the lakefront park, just opposite the church's entrance, rested something so out of place in Switzerland that I'll never forget it. It was a bust of George Washington. Yes, our George Washington of the United States of America. I was so perplexed by my find that I later read up on it to learn that George Washington had never stepped foot in Lugano, but a nineteenth-century Swiss entrepreneur who had made his fortune in the United States had donated the sculpture in honor of the land of opportunity across the ocean. I was touched by the Swiss sense of admiration and generosity, and I felt happy for our nation's first president that he had posthumously been given a home with a view of Lake Lugano.

Lunchtime had approached, and my stomach was letting me know it. Even beneath my many layers of clothing, I could actually hear it grumbling, so I headed back to Piazza della Riforma, planning on finding a warm café to nestle in and enjoy some lunch. But along my way, a street vendor advised me to check out the Gabbani delicatessen. Either I had the word *tourist* written across my forehead, or he worked for Gabbani. Maybe it was a bit of both.

Gabbani was located northwest of Piazza della Riforma, just off of Piazza Cioccaro. As soon as I stepped inside, I knew that I was right to have followed the voice of reason who had practically accosted me in the street. I indulged myself in a variety of Alpine cheeses, calling my meal an exotic Swiss lunch, and I finished it all off with enough chocolate pastries to satisfy the worst chocoholic.

After my lunch at Gabbani, I spent the remainder of my time in Lugano roaming some of the smaller streets between Piazza della Riforma and the train station. It was the first time in a long time that I felt free, independent, and responsible to no one. Then the dark thought hit me; it was how I would have felt if Enzo had never been born.

I stopped in my tracks before a storefront window and caught my reflection. *You are a horrible person*, it said, and then I played psychological devil's advocate. *Maybe all mothers have these thoughts at one time or another. It's okay for you to miss your freedom.* I prayed that my latter thoughts were true and headed quickly back to the train station, not wanting to enjoy any more frightening feelings of liberty. I was afraid that if given even one more moment of such pleasure, I might never return to my son.

During the early months of 1996, things changed a bit. Carlo was due to graduate that coming summer, and so he was studying particularly hard with the goal of being accepted into a doctoral program. I took the opportunity several times to suggest that he apply to an American university because it would greatly help his international marketability. He repeatedly reminded me that he had no desire to have international marketability; the European Union suited him just fine.

Having hired a baby-sitter, I had returned to work part-time since full-time contracts were never offered under the table, which was how I was being paid. After all, I lacked the work permit that had originally brought me to Bologna, and there was no way of acquiring a renewal without returning to the States...something which I had been indirectly forbidden to consider.

Since my return from Lugano back in December, I had taken it upon myself to initiate the process of obtaining permanent residency. The collection of the appropriate documents and the bureaucracy of the process prevented me from even applying until February, which meant that I would not see my official papers until July. This meant that I would either have to return to Lugano in June when my six-month tourist stay expired or stay in Bologna and take the risk that nothing went wrong between June and July. Though I longed to return to Lugano and had even suggested that Carlo and I go away together to celebrate his twenty-fifth birthday, the month of June passed us by without travel or incident.

In July, our little Mazzini family celebrated three important events: Enzo's first birthday, my twenty-fourth, and the arrival of my legal status as a permanent resident of Italy. In honor of the first event, I decided to make an overseas phone call. It was long overdue.

On a particularly humid July afternoon, I strolled with Enzo into the center of town and to the nearest tobacco stand, where they sold public phone calling cards. I then made my way to one of the open phone boxes, which was always hard to find but necessary since I couldn't fit Enzo's stroller into a closed booth. I took a deep breath and dialed the Gossett home in Miami, realizing that in Florida it was ten o'clock in the morning on a Monday—an unlikely time to find anyone home. But to my great surprise, my mother answered the phone. "Hello?"

Her voice immediately brought me to tears. "Hi, Mom." I tried to control the quiver of my voice. "It's Millie."

"Millie! Are you alright? Where are you?"

I could hear her crying too.

"I'm here in Bologna, and I'm so sorry for the past two years. If you can forgive me, I really need your help." My voice was so soft that I could barely hear myself above the street noise around me.

"Emilia Gossett, you are my daughter. And no matter how angry or hurt I have felt, I have always prayed for this day and have always known that I would forgive you. Please tell me what's wrong."

I must have cried for almost a minute into that public phone receiver before regaining enough control to tell my story. It was a good thing that I had purchased the most expensive calling card available and that Enzo had decided to take a catnap, because when I finished telling my story, it was Mom's turn to talk. "Please let me buy you a ticket home. I don't care how much it costs." I tried to protest, but she cut me off and continued outlining her plan. "I know you'd have to come without the baby, but you could look at it as a little vacation, which I'm sure you need. And while you're here, we'll see what we can do about fixing things up with Andrew's legal situation."

"Who?" She had lost me.

"The baby. I'm sorry, Sweetie, but your father and I can never remember the baby's name, so we call him Andrew."

"It's Enzo."

"Well, that sounds like Andrew, don't you think?"

I ignored her comment and attempted to resume the thread of our conversation. "I appreciate your efforts, Mom, but Enzo's Report of Birth Abroad Certificate has to be obtained here in Italy, and Carlo isn't willing to cooperate."

"Oh Millie, there must be something we can do from this end. You know, my friend, Sandra is politically connected. I'll bet she can help us. I'll call her as soon as I hang up with you. But first, I'll book you a ticket home for next week. How does that sound?"

"Mom, you're being so nice, especially since I don't deserve it, but I can't leave. And I'm afraid to go against Carlo. I'm not sure if he would be able to keep me from Enzo."

"Now how is that possible, Millie? You're the child's mother. Isn't that worth something in that country?"

"I don't know. My mother-in-law has an awesomely strong hold over her son, and her family is very politically connected. I don't know how this culture works or what she's capable of." Then I dared to ask the question which Carlo had told me to ask seven months earlier. "Is there any way that you and Dad could come and visit?"

"My God, it's been years since your father and I returned to Bologna!" She sounded nostalgic making her claim, and I hoped it was a good sign. "Let me talk to your father. He'll be a harder sell than me since he's been busy pointing his finger at everyone concerned in this matter; that is, when I can get him to even broach the topic of you, my dear."

It hurt me to hear such things, and I began to wonder why I had called. My silence must have resounded through the receiver because Mom changed her tune rather suddenly. "Now don't you worry, Millie. I'll make him come around. Twenty-six years ago, I talked your father into going to Bologna. I can do it again. I can talk your father into almost anything."

Though I wanted to have faith in her optimism, I felt lost. "I'm going to hang up now, Mom. Thanks for your support; I really needed it. Please send my love to Romy, and Dad too."

"I sure will, Sweetie. Keep your head up, and thanks for calling." She made kissing sounds into the receiver and then hung up.

I hung up my end of the line and looked down at Enzo, still sleeping peacefully in his stroller. Suddenly, I got the strangest urge to kick the stroller as hard as I could and rouse him from his contentment. Didn't he know that life sucked sometimes? I wanted to hear him crying so I'd know that he, too, was miserable. I felt angry and fed up with having someone else dictate my life. I missed the sense of control that had once carried me through my days with headstrong confidence. I wished that I hadn't been so naive when I returned to Bologna with a baby in my belly instead of staying put in Miami. And worst of all, I wished I would stop having this resentful train of thoughts, which had first reared its ugly head half a year ago in Switzerland.

CHAPTER 5

▼

I never kicked Enzo's stroller, and I still secretly pat myself on the back for not losing control. But I do often look back on that summer day in 1996 and wonder if there had been anything else I could possibly have done to prevent the events of the years that followed. I still don't know the answer.

My parents never came to visit me in Bologna. In fact, to this day, they have never returned. The place that had once held enough happy memories and nostalgia for them to name their two daughters in its honor has lost all meaning because of me. Because of me, my once open-minded parents can only see the dark stain that one family has left on an otherwise beautiful city. They talk poorly about Italians, forgetting that they once lived among them and loved that time in their lives. My parents do not understand how I can speak of Italy without spitting at the ground or tell my story to friends without cursing the Mazzini-Buonsignore name. Though I have felt hopeless at many times during the past nine years, I have secretly kept on believing that things would someday get better. My father calls me Blind Faith because he believes that's how I live my life. My mother lovingly calls me Job and tells me that my patience could be measured in biblical proportions. I tell them that they should instead call me Hope because that's the only thing that keeps me alive.

About three weeks after my phone conversation with my mother, I received a letter from Romy. The gist spoke of how my father would in no way consider meeting my husband and how my mother didn't have the courage to break the bad news to me. Romy went on to beg for my return to Florida. She told me to leave my schmuck of a husband behind and kidnap her nephew if I had to. She clearly had no idea of what the real world was like, and although I entertained her idea for a split second, I turned my focus back to my parents. They would never be visiting me in Bologna. Correspondence between Romy and me continued for the next several weeks as I suggested that Mom and Dad meet me in Rome. That way, they could meet Enzo and avoid seeing Carlo. I was sure that I could get away to Rome without much argument, but Romy only reported that my father refused to spend so much money for a clandestine visit. I wrote back that meeting his grandson would be priceless. She wrote back that my father was now angry at her for meddling. I decided to face the fact that my father's avoidance had less to do with Carlo and more to do with me. They say that there's no vengeance like a woman scorned, but they never speak of a father whose heart has been broken by his first-born daughter…irrevocable damage, for sure.

At this point, I will fast-forward through the next year. Carlo was accepted to the doctoral program (another three years of study), I was able to establish a teaching contract since becoming a permanent resident, Enzo learned to walk and talk a bit, and Carlo and I grew angrier with each other. I continued to push the naturalization issue, and Carlo continued to resist. When I would challenge him on it, he would question my loyalty to our family. When I begged my computer scientist husband to bring Internet access into our home so I could maintain contact with my family, he refused. When I accused him of holding me prisoner in his country, he reminded me that I was free to leave. And when he started coming home very early in the mornings (instead of very late at night), I accused him of fooling around. He responded by turning my argument on its head and suggesting that I, too, was playing the field while he was busy studying. He said that he had noticed some very good-looking students of mine flirting with me after class. I accused him of spying on me, and he said that my anger confirmed his suspicions.

That is mostly how our conversations played out again and again throughout the year. I don't dare mention how they went if Regina entered the picture. Suffice it to say that the bond I had felt that day in her kitchen with the ultrasound photo was held together with nothing more than a piece of silly putty. On the day of Enzo's baptism, Regina had resumed her role as my opponent. Whenever Carlo mentioned her in his arguments, it was all I could do to avoid smacking him in the jaw and running away as fast as my legs would carry me.

As the summer of 1997 drew near, I didn't think I could stand the heat any more, and then I received a letter from Romy telling me that our father had suffered a mild heart attack. I phoned my mother and asked her to book me a ticket to Miami right after Enzo's birthday. My father's ailing health was the impetus that I needed to convince myself to take a break. I had also convinced myself that, by being state side, maybe there was something I could do to help Enzo obtain a U.S. passport.

On July 1, 1997, we celebrated Enzo's second birthday in my favorite park in Bologna, Giardini Margherita. Apart from Carlo's mamma and the cousins, our guests included two other families: one belonging to a colleague of mine, and the other belonging to Carlo's mentor at the university. Both families had young children and were, sadly enough, the only way that Carlo and I could provide children at Enzo's birthday party. It seemed we both had done a poor job at forging friendships, perhaps for fear of bringing inno-cent strangers into our messed up world.

The day after Enzo's birthday, I left for Miami but not before spending a quiet morning with my son. I awoke at five o'clock, planning on having some private time to shower and get myself together emotionally more than anything else. As I looked at myself in the bathroom mirror, I realized that it was my twenty-fifth birth-day. I studied my face and scrutinized its flaws, but I decided there were too many to worry about on this morning of my big trip. I was stepping into the shower when I heard a little voice in the bathroom doorway.

"Mamma! *Bagiono!*" Enzo's attempt at the good-morning greet-ing of *buongiorno* always made me smile. I bent down to hug my boy, but he pushed me away and tore off his pajamas and then his wet diaper, leaving both items on the bathroom floor. "Mamma! Shaya wif you!"

Everything was an exclamation with Enzo, and as he pointed to the shower and then began to climb into the tub, I knew that I would have no privacy this morning. I didn't care. A little voice in the back of my mind told me to cherish this moment that we were having together. It would probably be the best birthday present I was going to receive that year.

As Enzo and I showered together on my birthday, I watched him trying to be a big boy. He would look up at me and then try to copy what I was doing. I had given him the baby bath soap to work with so that when he tried to shampoo his own hair but forgot to close his eyes, there would be no tears. As his little body got soapier and soapier, he looked like a fluffy cloud with an angel's face peering out.

"You're Mamma's little cloud angel!"

Enzo smiled from ear to ear. "Make wigs, Mamma!" He tried to look over his own shoulder.

"Wings. All right, let me see what I can do here." I turned him around and began my work. I reached out of the shower and managed to find two washcloths, which I first soaked and then rested on Enzo's shoulders. Then I loaded up the washcloths with the remaining soap from the bottle of baby bath until a nice head of foam had formed. I had to keep Enzo out of the shower's spray so as to preserve the wings as long as possible. As soon as I finished, I carefully lifted up my soapy cloud angel and stepped out of the shower, soaking wet. I held Enzo up to see his reflection in the mirror, turning him a bit so he could see the wings, but by the time I had him in the right position, the wings had already melted away. "I'm sorry, Sweetie. I made your wings but they flew away."

"*Va bene.*" It's all right.

That was my Enzo. He had been blessed with a good nature that always seemed to let him bounce back from disappointment. Even at two years old, that much was apparent.

I dried off Enzo and then myself as he sat on the bathroom floor, seeming to examine me.

"I'm really going to miss you, my little cloud angel."

He looked confused.

"I'm going on a vacation today to see my own Mamma and Babbo. They live very far away, so I'll be gone for a while. But then I'll come back to see you, and we'll do lots of fun things this summer. You'll stay with Babbo and Nonna. And I'll call you every day, *Va bene?*"

"*Va be'.*" Okay.

Enzo stood up and hugged my legs tightly. I could feel his soft skin enveloping me, and I wished I could remain his prisoner forever. I bent down and kissed the top of his head as I rubbed my hands through his damp curls. Then I glanced at my watch, resting on the sink counter, and realized that I had to get moving if I was going to catch my flight. I hated the idea of telling Enzo that he had to let go, but before I could say a word, he had released me. The last image I remember is his bare bottom waddling down the hallway towards the salon as he shouted, "*Ciao, Mamma!*"

I awoke Carlo just before my taxi was due to arrive. "Enzo's been up for a while. He's had breakfast and even a bath."

"What? Why?"

I did love the childlike breathiness of Carlo's sleepy voice, and for the first time since my mother had booked my ticket, I thought I might actually miss him. "Don't worry about it," I told him as I sat on the edge of the bed. "But you need to get up now because I have to go."

Carlo sat up in the bed and shot a glance at the clock on the nightstand. "*Va bene.* Mamma will be here in an hour anyway."

"You can't be alone with your son for more than one hour?" Although I knew that now was not the time to pick a fight, the mere mention of Regina always made me a bit crazy, for sure.

"Millie. Mamma says she needs to talk with me…kind of like a family pow-wow."

"Strange timing," I pointed out. "I won't be here, and I'm part of this family. Why would she wait until I was gone to have her pow-wow?" I could feel my own mocking expression at Carlo's choice of vocabulary, but I didn't care how I sounded.

"I don't know." He pronounced each word slowly and deliberately.

I stood up abruptly and started to leave. "I've left my return flight information on the kitchen counter, and I'll call you as soon as I'm in Miami, which should be around ten o'clock this evening Bologna time. Maybe you can fill me in on the pow-wow when I call." I hoped my sarcasm was evident.

"When are you coming back, Millie?" Carlo asked the question as if we had never discussed my trip at all. I stopped in the bedroom doorway and turned to look at him, not sure what the hidden message in his tone could be.

"You know I'm coming back in two weeks, on the sixteenth."

"So you're not leaving me. You will come back."

They were statements more than questions. As much as I would have loved to have been able to stay in Miami and never deal with Carlo or Regina again, I would never have been able to leave Enzo behind. I would rather have shared my prison with Enzo than lived alone in freedom.

"Carlo." I decided to ignore the direction of his comments and give him the chance to wish me a happy birthday so that we could depart on a good note. "Before I go, do you have anything else to say to me...on July second?"

He looked at me knowingly and then smiled the cruelest smile I have ever seen. "Have a safe trip, Millie."

CHAPTER 6

▼

Dear Millie,

I'm sorry that Enzo was sleeping when you called, and I'm sorry that I wasn't able to fill you in over the phone about my meeting with Mamma. She suggested that I'd be able to explain things better in a letter and said that I should make myself very clear about where things stand, so I'll get right to the point.

These past few years have definitely been tough on both of us, and I've tried my hardest to do the right thing and to work hard for our family. Unfortunately, I don't feel that you have made the same efforts. You were careless about your legal status, which I believe you did in order to avoid working as hard as I do. And you were unwilling to let our son become a part of his own culture by making such a big deal about his baptism. I believe your attitude towards my country is not appropriate for my son, who is Italian and always will be. You have been trying for years to leave Italy, with your references to getting an American passport for Enzo, so that you can take him out of the country without me. And I also must mention that your loyalty to our marriage is highly questionable, since I know you flirt with your students and only God knows what else.

Now that you have decided to leave Enzo and me because you so badly needed a "vacation" from the beautiful family I've tried so hard to create for you, I feel that it would be best if you did not return to Bolo-

gna. Mamma has offered to take care of Enzo and become the positive role model that he needs to succeed in Italian society. She is very well-connected and will provide a loving home for him while I dedicate myself to my doctoral studies and career, which I would have been able to do more efficiently if I hadn't been working so hard for you.

I don't mean to sound threatening, but if you try to return to Bologna, you will be faced with legal problems because you have been accused of attempting to kidnap my son and take him across the Italian border without my permission. I know this may sound cruel to you, and I'm sorry things had to be handled this way, but you chose to leave us. There is a price to be paid for all bad decisions in life. I wish you good luck in your country, and I hope you can find the happiness that you have been lacking here in Italy. Please know that Mamma will take wonderful care of Enzo.

Sincerely,
Carlo

I don't know how many times I had read the letter before, but with each reading, the shock remained. It started when a courier hand-delivered the letter to my parents' door only ten days into my stay in Miami. Before opening the envelope, I could not help but wonder how much it had cost Carlo to send the letter via overseas courier. What was so important that it couldn't wait until my return? Then I panicked, imagining the worst for Enzo, so I quickly opened the envelope and read the letter while still standing in the doorway. When I finished reading, I was sure that something had gotten lost in translation because the words made no sense to me. I wasn't really sure what had happened. So I sat down on the sofa, curled my legs up beneath myself, and read again...and again...and again.

Sometimes, life gives you moments that seem so surreal that you are forced to challenge them; they cannot possibly be happening, or you have completely misinterpreted their meaning. Either way, you refuse to believe that time hasn't stood still and that you have actually lost several minutes of your life trying to stop the clock. The brain works at breakneck speed (and almost actually breaks your neck as you crane your head in confusion), and you do not even realize how your heart rate has accelerated until you notice beads of sweat dripping from your forehead and into your eyes.

As I was wiping away the salty perspiration that was so badly stinging my eyes, my father walked into the room. The past week had been good for us as a lot of water under the bridge had been pushed downstream. Dad had been the one trying to help me at the office of the Immigration and Naturalization Service and even the Italian consulate as I petitioned unsuccessfully for Enzo's naturalization. (American law stated that he had to be present.) We were talking again though some tension still lingered.

"Are you crying? Are you all right, Millie?"

I looked at him blankly. "I'm not crying; I'm sweating."

"Well, the air is on. Are you sick?"

"Yes." I handed him the letter, knowing that although I shouldn't really have burdened him with the stress, I couldn't handle it alone. My father sat down in the arm chair opposite the sofa and read the letter. I believed that by unloading the letter from my hands, I had somehow unloaded the burden of its contents, but I was still sweating as if I had just run a marathon.

"I don't understand this. Is it true, Millie?"

"Is what true?" I didn't understand his question.

"Did you try to kidnap Enzo from Carlo?"

He really asked me that question. I didn't answer him right away because I was flashing back to the thought crime of kidnapping, which I had indeed committed, and I felt like a character in George Orwell's *1984*. I actually began to wonder if, in some other dimension, I had already been tried for the crimes in my head and found guilty by an Italian jury. I brought myself back to 1997 to see my father's frightened expression, and I suddenly remembered the terrible question that he had just posed. I felt my anger soar, and I yelled at the one man who was supposed to have faith in me. "No, Dad! I did not try to kidnap my son! It's all a lie! Pure fabrication!"

"That's a serious story to fabricate."

His doubt stung me almost worse than the letter that he still held in his hands. My father's American mindset would not be able to accept the world of the Mediterranean cultures, where it was not *what* you know but rather *who* you know that could provide a person with unyielding power. "It's different over there. My mother-in-law knows important people who can find ways to make my problems very legal and very legitimate. Carlo may not have explained the events as thoroughly as they've transpired, but trust me, Dad. I happen to know that Carlo has an uncle who is an immigration attorney in Rome, and he worked on the police force, giving him very strong government ties. Regina has made sure that everything has been handled in a manner that will prevent my return."

"Millie, that's insane. This is 1997. Governments don't run that way anymore."

"Which governments are you talking about, Dad?" I couldn't help but look at him with the eyes of a parent scrutinizing her naïve child. "Anyway," I continued. "There's something else very important that Carlo didn't mention in his letter."

"What's that?"

"That I'm Jewish. He apparently didn't have the courage to reveal his mother's hidden wildcard; she hates me because I'm Jewish. I'm sure my religion helped her pull the necessary strings to have this crime reported against me."

"But that's discrimination!" My father stood up as he shouted.

I could only look at him with envy for having made it into his fifties with such innocence in tact, but as my envy quickly turned to pity, I stood up and walked out of the room. I needed to be alone.

My parents wanted to take legal action, but it was Romy who had turned out to be the voice of reason. At times my worst enemy in childhood and at times my best friend, my sister had stepped up to the plate with a human approach to my problem. Three days after receiving Carlo's letter, I was seated on an airplane, reading the letter's distressing news yet another time as Romy slept in the seat next to mine on the American Airlines flight to Milan.

Our plan was to first call Carlo's bluff. If he wouldn't let me near Enzo, then Romy would be there to do my leg work for me. She would confront Carlo on a human level and hopefully have the opportunity to check up on Enzo by being bold enough to pay a visit to Regina. Romy had promised that she was up to the task, and I believed her. Almost worse than me, my younger sister had an innate sense of drama about her. The only thing that had stopped her from crossing the ocean as I had was her devotion to her graduate studies in psychology, which she had just begun one year earlier. Romy loved the study of the mind and was on a sure-footed path to becoming a Ph.D. When faced with my dilemma, Romy decided to take on Carlo as her first unknowing patient. My only fear was that Regina would do a head job on Romy quicker than my sister could say xenophobia.

Once on the ground in Milan, Romy and I quickly made our way to the passport checkpoint since we were both traveling with only carry-on bags. I was nervous about my pending problems in Bologna and didn't even notice that Romy had passed through Customs first without incident. She stepped away from the counter and waited for me to pass through. My head was somewhere else, but I approached the Customs agent and tried to look confident and nonchalant at the same time. I said *Buongiorno* as I slid my passport across the counter. The agent mumbled a return greeting and then scanned my passport through a machine. It beeped twice, and the agent looked up at me in surprise. "*Signora,* please come with me."

I sat in the Customs office, stripped of my passport and my courage. As I awaited my judgment, the panicked expression on Romy's face as I was quickly escorted away from the line stuck in my head. I was simply stunned. I don't know how long I sat alone in that office before a Customs agent returned, accompanied by Romy.

I boldly asked the agent why I was being detained. After all, I was an American citizen, free to visit Italy whenever I wanted, wasn't I? He scanned the computer printout and turned to face me. "The attempted kidnapping conviction would be the problem." My jaw dropped open, and Romy threw a hand over her mouth. The agent only looked further down his nose at me. "I don't know about America, but in Italy, we take the protection of our children quite seriously."

"May I please see the paper?" I asked timidly.

The agent handed me the printout, which spelled out my story rather clearly. It even referred to a Family Court order prohibiting my contact with Enzo and giving sole custody to Carlo. A police report file number corroborated the charge and classified my file as a conviction.

I was enraged. "The whole thing was fabricated! I was never charged with such a crime and certainly never convicted. I wasn't even in Italy to stand trial!"

The Customs agent showed no expression on his face as he repeated the charge. "Convicted of attempted kidnapping."

There was a moment of silence as my wheels were spinning, trying to come up with a plausible reason to delay my inevitable deportation. Then Romy spoke for the first time. "Could it be a computer error? Isn't that possible?"

The agent looked at her in disgust. "Do you think that Italy is so far behind the United States that we can't get our computer systems in order?"

"It's a fair question," I piped up. "We just want to know if it's possible that a mistake has been made since the rest of my life depends on it."

"That is not my job to determine, *Signora*."

Exasperated, I slumped into the plastic-molded chair and began to whimper. The agent must have sensed my discomfort at having an emotional breakdown in front of a complete stranger, and he walked out of the room.

Romy quickly came to my side and hugged me. "What do you want me to do, Millie?"

She sounded scared, but I knew that I had to hand her the reins, or else I would be lost forever. "I need you to go on to Bologna. Find me some paper and I'll draw up a little map with directions to a hotel, my apartment, and even Regina's apartment. You've got to talk to Carlo, and you must see Enzo for me."

Romy nodded her head and ran out of the office in search of paper and pen. When she returned, I jotted down as much as I could, feeling rushed since I knew that she had a train to catch. We didn't exchange many words as I wrote quickly. I handed her the paper, hugged her tightly, and pushed her out the office door and into the airport terminal.

I don't care to recount the details of my stay in the custody of the Customs agent's office. I will just tell you that I remained there for a few hours until the airline could confirm a seat for me on the next returning flight to Miami, which would leave that same afternoon. As I was escorted onto the plane by two agents and others looked on with curiosity, I pretended that I was an aristocratic dignitary and that the agents were actually my security guards. That was the only way I could make it through the moment with my head held high.

Romy was freaked out when Customs took me away, but she gathered her courage and followed my instructions, catching the train to Bologna. Feeling nervous, scared, and excited at the same time, she watched everything outside the window and tried to imagine what my life had been like living in that country.

When the train pulled into Bologna's station, it was a beautiful afternoon, and Romy was sure that the good weather was a positive sign that things would go her way. She followed the map I had given her and went to the hotel to get settled. She then headed out to my apartment to find Carlo, but nobody's name was on the intercom name plate for my unit, strangely enough. She buzzed and buzzed, but no one answered. She stopped an approaching resident of my building, who was kind enough to speak to her in broken English and inform her that Signore Mazzini had moved out two days ago. Romy quickly thanked him and headed straight for Regina's apartment, sure that she would find Carlo there.

When Romy buzzed Regina's place, Carlo answered. She announced herself as a colleague of mine who was worried because she hadn't seen me this summer. He said that I had returned to the States and wouldn't be coming back. As I had instructed, Romy said that she had a late birthday gift for Enzo and asked if she could come up. Hesitating for a moment, Carlo buzzed her through the door.

When Carlo opened the door, Romy could instantly see how I could lose my mind over him. But then she reminded herself of what an asshole he was and regained her composure. She asked him if they could talk in private, not sure if Regina was in the apartment, and he said that they were alone. So she came clean.

"I'm not actually a colleague of Millie's. I'm your sister-in-law, Romy Gossett."

Carlo practically swallowed his tongue. "Where is Millie?"

"She won't be bothering you since she was virtually arrested in Milan," Romy retorted. Carlo looked as if he felt very guilty and didn't say much for a moment, so Romy pulled out Enzo's present. "Can I please meet my nephew?"

Without Regina in the house, Carlo seemed scared of Romy. He kept looking at the clock as if he was hoping his mamma would come home soon. Romy was actually scared that Regina would and wanted to get down to business as quickly as possible. But first she had to see Enzo.

Enzo was in the salon, watching television. He looked up when Romy came in, and he smiled as if he recognized her. Then he got serious. It was as if he was expecting someone else and was disappointed to see that he was mistaken. Romy went over to Enzo and introduced herself, but it didn't faze him. So she gave my son the present. He opened it up and was very excited to find the teddy bear that I had bought him.

"It's really from your mamma," Romy said softly.

"You know Mamma?" Enzo asked.

"Yes," she told him. "I'm Mamma's sister. I'm your Aunt Romy. I live in Miami, where Mamma is from. In fact," she added, "I saw Mamma just yesterday and she wanted me to tell you that she loves you more than anything and misses you so much."

At that point, Carlo came in and asked Romy to leave Enzo alone and come into the kitchen. He had a very serious tone that kind of scared her, so she obeyed. "Why are you here?" Carlo asked.

"Why are you doing this to Millie, to Enzo's mamma?" Romy felt brave.

"You have no idea what went on, and there is nothing you can do to change things."

Now, Romy felt bold. "You are totally unreasonable and so irrational that I can't see what my sister ever saw in you."

Carlo fought back. "You are sticking your nose in where it doesn't belong and are completely out of your element." Romy flinched, and Carlo added, "Millie's stuff has been shipped back to Miami and will probably arrive in a couple of months. Now, would you please leave?"

Romy needed to get her head together and formulate another plan, so she left but not before shouting good-bye to Enzo.

She was exhausted after all that travel and the confrontation with Carlo, so she ended up sleeping the rest of the afternoon and right into the morning. The next day, she walked around a bit in the morning and finally had the chance to see the Italian city that everyone else in my family knows so well. She roamed around, trying to gather the courage to make her way back to the apartment in hopes of finding Regina.

Luck was on Romy's side when she buzzed in because Regina answered this time. At first, Romy thought the woman wouldn't let her up, but when Romy said that she wasn't going away, Regina buzzed her through. Romy realized that Carlo wasn't around when Regina opened the door to greet her. She was surprisingly cordial as she invited my sister into the salon and offered her some coffee, which Romy accepted. She wanted to be as polite as possible to get on Regina's good side, even though I had said that was virtually impossible. It took Regina a long time to return with the coffee, but eventually she reappeared with a beautiful hostess tray and set out an impressive display.

"You look a lot like Millie." Regina's first words as she poured coffee into Romy's waiting cup.

"Thank you. I take that as a great compliment."

That's when Regina began the attack. "Well, for a Jewish girl, Millie is very attractive."

Romy put down her coffee cup, aware that such a comment could come out of my mother-in-law's mouth since I had given my sister fair warning. "Why did you arrange for Millie's conviction?" Romy cut right to the chase.

Regina acted surprised. "What conviction?"

"Millie has been convicted of attempted kidnapping. How did you do that? Why would you do that?" Romy was perplexed.

"We didn't have her convicted…only charged."

"Well, you must not know the power of your own corruption," Romy said.

"I would never go that far," Regina sneered.

"Then, clear it up for her."

Regina looked Romy over once before responding. "However the conviction got on record is a mystery to me. Maybe it means that Millie was really not meant to be a part of this family anymore. That's what she wanted anyway…to get away from us. You should tell your sister to be careful what she wishes for."

Romy was so enraged and had no idea of how to respond, so instead she posed a different question to Regina. "Why do you hate Jews so much?"

Without missing a beat, Regina asked, "Do you really want to know?"

"That's why I asked," Romy responded.

"I'll tell you, but if you say anything to Carlo, I'll deny every word."

"All right," Romy agreed.

"Carlo's father was a Jew."

Romy thought she was going to stop breathing right there. Regina must have taken the silence as respectful listening because she went on. "He didn't care much for religion, so it never became an issue in our family. But in Enzo's family, it was another story. They were very successful hotel owners in Rimini, and they were rather upset that Enzo had married out of the religion. They never accepted me, and they were miserly with their riches." Regina scrunched her brow in disapproval. "As a result, things were tight for Enzo and me since his family kept him down in the business, like some sort of punishment. My family is also successful, but I didn't want to ask them for money. When I became a widow, however, I had to go to my family for support because the Mazzini family basically cut me out of their lives, like some cancer that had burdened them for so many years. They were cruel people who only cared about their own kind, and even though Carlo was their flesh and blood, they cut him off too." Regina stopped and took a sip of her coffee. Then she added one more comment. "Carlo doesn't know that his father was a Jew, and I intend on keeping it that way. He should never have to be shamed into being associated with such selfish and heartless people." Regina looked at my sister as if implicating her for all Jewish crimes against non-Jews.

"I understand your pain, *Signora*," Romy began. "But my sister is not that kind of person."

"They're all that kind of person, young lady," Regina retorted.

Romy didn't think it was the time to lecture on stereotyping and tolerance, so she opted for self-defense. "My family is not like that. The Gossett family understands tolerance." She couldn't resist throwing the word out there. "And my sister would never have done to Carlo what he has done to her. Not in the name of God or anyone else." Regina looked like she wanted to say something, but Romy kept on talking. "It's a good thing that the Gossetts don't form such stereotypes as you have, or else we would think that it was actually all the Italians who were cruel and heartless."

Regina didn't say anything. She just gathered up the serving tray and walked into the kitchen. In a low voice, she called out to Romy. "You may leave now."

Three days after my return from Italy, Romy sat in the living room, looking rather helpless before Mom, Dad, and me. "I'm sorry, Millie. I know I didn't come close to accomplishing anything."

"It's all right," I told her. "I'm not sure there was really anything to accomplish. But at least I now know Regina's big secret. Maybe I can somehow use it against her."

"I don't know, Millie. She'll deny it and say that you're making it up."

"But what if I could somehow find the Mazzinis in Rimini? They'd be able to confirm it, right?"

"Maybe," Mom jumped in. "But hatred is powerful. For all we know, the Mazzini family is as miserly and cruel as Regina says."

"But Mom, we're M.O.T."

My mother looked perplexed, but Romy came to her rescue. "Members of the Tribe, Mom." Then Romy looked over at my father and said, "Dad's an honorary member."

My father laughed, and it was the tension break that we all so desperately needed.

After Romy's return from Bologna, I tried calling Carlo many times a day, but I always got the answering machine. I left messages, including some directed at Enzo in case the calls were being screened and Enzo might have been able to hear my voice, but Carlo never returned my calls. My parents consulted an immigration attorney, but it appeared that legally I had no recourse. I had willingly left Italy, and my attempted kidnapping charge appeared to be legally documented.

Though I was not particularly savvy on the Internet, I realized that my next task was to surf the net and find the Rimini Mazzinis. I knew that they worked in the hotel industry, and it was a simple enough task to connect the Mazzini name with a hotel. The harder part came when I had to contact the hotel and get the Mazzini owner to acknowledge the Buonsignore connection. The family was not so willing to cooperate. They had enjoyed over twenty years of Bologna-free hassles and had no desire to involve themselves in a family dispute. They did not speak very highly of their lost son, brother, or cousin, and I decided that bringing them into the picture would only feed the fire of Jewish hatred which burned so fervently in Regina. For the time being, my hope was lost.

As the summer months passed, Romy and I would sit in our bedroom and fantasize about such ideas as obtaining a false passport for Enzo and hiring smugglers to kidnap him and bring him to Miami. I figured that if I had already been convicted of the crime, why not reap the benefits? We even fantasized about Romy being the kidnapper. Our talks eventually turned from fantasy to my own obsession with getting my son back. I will confess that, at the risk of being discovered by the FBI, I actually did some research into how to get Enzo a false passport. The nastier task would be finding a smuggler to enter the country with Enzo's passport in her possession (I figured it would have to be a woman to make it more believable to authorities) and successfully get a hold of him without creating a scene. When I then tried to guess how much such a crime would cost, I instead imagined Aunt Romy approaching Enzo and telling him that she would bring him to Mamma, but the idea of having my sister incarcerated in addition to losing my son was unthinkable.

By the time Labor Day rolled around, I had found out exactly how to obtain the false passport for Enzo. Unfortunately, I had also come to realize that I didn't have the courage necessary to commit the even larger criminal act that would have to follow. It had been two months since I had seen Enzo or heard his voice. I had been so wrapped up in my clandestine planning that it had been enough to prevent me from falling into a depression, but now, my planning was over. I would have to find another method of saving Enzo.

By that autumn of 1997, Romy had returned to school at Florida International University to continue her graduate studies. She was due to graduate in December and had already been accepted into the doctoral program for January. Watching her have such direction in her life with no outside obligations really brought me down. She was so free and so dedicated to something that she loved doing. While she headed off to the university each morning bright and early, I slept in until at least eleven o'clock every day, much to my parents' frustration. They had been nagging me since the end of summer to look for a job and even encouraging Romy and me to get our own apartment. They reminded me that no matter what was going wrong in my life, I was an adult who should be supporting myself and doing my best to move on.

How does a parent tell a child who has just lost her own child to move on? I wondered if my parents would have moved on if I had disappeared from their lives. Then I thought of my Aunt Elizabeth who had lost her eleven-year-old daughter to cancer. I guess she had moved on even though I still perceived her as a woman in permanent mourning. Maybe that was how I was meant to live my life…in permanent mourning. But my case was vastly different because my child was alive. My child would grow up and have a life without me, probably having been told that I had abandoned him or even died. How was I supposed to go about my days knowing that every minute I was away from Enzo, he would be growing further and further out of my reach? Already, months had passed since I showered with him on my birthday, which made me realize that I would never enjoy another birthday again. The memory of that morning with Enzo would bring on enough nostalgia to wash away any feelings of celebration.

My clothing and other personal belongings from Bologna arrived in early October, and as I sifted through everything, I thought I could smell Enzo. Carlo had included everything in the shipment except for the photo albums. It appeared that the only keepsake of Enzo that I would have were the three photos that had traveled with me to Miami in the first place. In the first picture, Enzo was eight months old, looking up at the camera in surprise. In the second, he was celebrating his first birthday and eating cake for the first time. And in the third, taken one month before my departure, he's actually posing for me, standing sure-footed with his hands on his hips and flashing his dazzling smile.

I was on my second day of trying to organize my things when my mother came into the bedroom and sat down on my bed. "Your father and I have been talking," she began. "We think you need to take some active steps to get on with your life. We're not saying to completely forget Enzo. In fact, I think you should continue pleading with Carlo and attempting to make contact in the hopes that someday you'll wear him down. He must have a human side, right?"

I shrugged my shoulders.

"Anyway, if you do get Enzo back some day, what good will you be to him if you can't support him? Take this unwanted time that has been given to you, and develop your career. You had once said that you wanted to go to graduate school. Dad and I will pay for it if you're willing to dedicate yourself to helping yourself."

"I will get Enzo back some day," I mumbled.

"What, Sweetie?"

"It's not *if* I get Enzo back but *when* I get him back. I will get my son back some day."

"All right then." Mom stood up. "Let's get your life in order so you'll be the best mother you can be to him."

"You're right," I said, even though my mother had already left the room. "After all, I am Enzo's mamma."

Part II
Matthew

CHAPTER 1

▼

I'm a Syracuse boy. Always have been, always will be. But I've been stuck in Florida since I was about twelve, and I'm afraid I'll be stuck here interminably, now that I'm at a Florida university, entangled in the spidery network of Floridian connections. I've really got to learn Spanish, but my heart fights with my head almost daily, telling it that you can do just fine in Syracuse without Spanish. Sure, living down here has some advantages: no snow tires to mess with, no roads to shovel in winter, great beaches. But I've been to the beach too many times already, and I'll take the first snowfall of the season over Biscayne Bay any day. When God drops that white blanket over you as night falls, it feels like you're being tucked into bed by Mother Nature herself.

Anyway, the poet in me can't seem to forget the North, pinning me against my parents, who love Florida and plan on spending the rest of their days here in God's waiting room. My sister is my only ally in this world of sticky days and balmy nights. She's had a rough time growing up here...got into some trouble in high school, the kind of trouble where you're lucky when you end up in a rehab center instead of prison. She's moved beyond that, but I know she believes that if we'd stayed in Syracuse, none of that shit would have happened. Who knows? Anyway, we have a little race on to see who will be the first to return to Syracuse and send news back to the pathetic soul left behind.

I must sound depressive, but I'm really not that kind of guy. These are just the thoughts that come to mind when someone asks me where I'm from because I don't like saying Florida. The truth of the matter is that I know I could have left sooner if it had meant that much to me. I could have shirked my unspoken obligation to go to a Florida college and applied for financial aid or scholarships to Syracuse, but I didn't. I work hard at the university, and I'm a smart guy, which I'm not afraid to admit. When you're blessed with a talent, you've got to love it, own it, and let it help you in this world. I love science, and I'm good at it. And I love living, which I think I'm pretty good at too, even here in Florida. I don't spend too much time brooding over location because this may sound crazy, but despite my desire to return to the North, I've always thought that here in the South, something important is going to happen to me…or some one.

Saturday, July 1, 2000. It was the new millennium, and everything had gone off without a hitch despite the projected nightmares of Y2K and the religious zealots' predictions of Armageddon. Strangely, as I sat peacefully at the News Café in South Beach, Florida, I wished the zealots had been right. For me, the past three years had been a taste of Hell, and I now felt so acclimated to the feeling that I would just as soon be there. It was my son's fifth birthday, and I had no idea what he was doing. I was sure that he had no memory of me, and I wondered what his father had told him about my absence. Was I the terrible witch who had abandoned him, or was I dead? I had come out to the beach early that morning so I could look across the ocean and imagine a summer afternoon in Bologna where Enzo would be celebrating his birthday. Was he surrounded by many friends? Was he a likable child? Was he happy?

I looked out across Ocean Drive and over the low barrier wall that separated the sidewalk from the sand. Several yards farther out, I could see the ocean, with its small, capless waves. In the wintertime, small white caps usually crested with the tide, but in July that rarely happened. Still, you could always find surfers attempting to ride the small, California wannabe waves, and this day was no exception. The beach was packed with hard bodies and not-so-hard bodies because not even the thick, humid, South Florida air could keep people away from the sun. As I watched the lunatics baking in their makeshift oven, I looked up at the several ceiling fans blowing on high speed above me, and I thanked them. Their warm air blew around me, and I imagined Enzo here with me at the beach. He would most likely want to be one of the beach babies, and I would be one of those responsible mothers who slather their children from scalp to toe with number forty-five sunscreen, sending my slimy sapling out to play in the sticky sand.

It had been three years since Enzo ran down the hallway and yelled *Ciao* before I flew away from him. Three long years based on the following routine: phone Regina's house every Saturday and Sunday morning in the hopes of getting a response on the other end of the phone line; write an entry in my journal every Sunday night before going to bed to tell Enzo about my week and how much I'm thinking about him; go to work Monday morning and try to pretend that I am a happy and successful university instructor who can make it through another painful week of life.

Despite the rigmarole of my days, I had been quite busy those past three years as I attempted to get my career in order. In 1999, I graduated from Florida International University, also known as FIU, with my Master's Degree in TESOL from the College of Education, which meant that I could teach at the same university in their program of English for Speakers of Other Languages. I worked part-time for four months until I was fortunate enough to be given a full-time position as of January, 2000. The New Year had so far proven to be a good year for me professionally as I built my nest egg, which I hoped to someday use to support Enzo when Judgment Day came to the Buonsignore-Mazzini household. Since I did pretty much nothing more than work and party on Saturday nights, my nest egg was slowly growing quite large. I was renting my own apartment in the city of Coral Gables, which was about a twenty-minute car ride to FIU. I used to share an apartment with Romy, but she got married in November of 1999. Her husband, David, was the director of an art gallery on South Beach, so they relocated there just after the wedding. The good news was that now I could spend the weekend on the beach whenever I wanted and have somewhere to go "home" to while I was there. Romy and David were very good to me and practically considered me one of their roommates during the weekend. They had a very busy social calendar, which had them out of the apartment most of the weekend. Their schedule essentially gave me free reign of my home away from home since I, in contrast, had no personal obligations of which to speak, though it had not always been that way.

Two years earlier, while still studying at FIU, the brother of one of my classmates fell in love with me, to put it bluntly. His name was Matthew Crane. His twin sister, Haley, was my classmate in our Curriculum Development course, which was a weekend module that met every Saturday from nine o'clock in the morning until four o'clock in the afternoon. We were given a lunch break for thirty minutes, and it was during that very first lunch break on the very first Saturday of our course that Haley and I became fast friends.

That's not an expression I use lightly, because I have never been the kind of person who makes a fast friend. My spirit is adventurous, but my manner is not as bold when forging new friendships with girls. I think that growing up with Romy, who was always my best friend and always more extroverted than I was, gave me the comfort of believing that I didn't need many other friends outside of my sister. That belief negatively affected my time in Bologna because I had lost the ability to befriend women. Yet, I had virtually cut my sister off at the same time. What a confusing time in my life, now that I look back at it. But let me return to Haley Crane.

During that first lunch break in August of 1998, Haley sat next to me and initiated idle small talk about the class and the instructor. I responded appropriately, as it's always easy to comment on your first impression of a new instructor and it gives you an instant bond with someone who you've only known for three hours. From the start, I knew that Haley was a kindred spirit because she seemed to guard her own sad secret that tormented her from day to day. We warmed to each other immediately and exchanged telephone numbers under the guise of being in contact regarding class matters.

On the second Saturday, while Haley and I were eating in the cafeteria, Matthew approached our table and sat down without invitation. Haley introduced us immediately, and Matthew offered his right hand in greeting. When I shook it, Matthew's expression changed subtly, and his grip on my hand lingered a bit longer than necessary. He was a good-looking man, though I didn't really see him as a man. I was twenty-six years old that summer, and Matthew was twenty-three, the same age that Carlo was when he and I had met back in 1994. With the life that I had led since that time and the heavy weight that I carried on my shoulders each day, I felt very much like Matthew's senior by more than just three years. To me, he was a boy, though certainly a very attractive and confident one.

Matthew looked exactly like Haley, with straight, dark blond hair and green eyes that turned down slightly at the corners, kind of a reverse image of my own almond-shaped eyes which seemed to turn up. But Matthew's mannerism was different from his twin's. His demeanor told the world that he knew what he wanted and could do anything necessary to achieve it. He wasn't arrogant but rather comfortable in his own skin, which was a rare gift in my opinion.

On the Sunday after that Saturday meeting, Matthew called to ask me out on a date. It was as if he were speaking a foreign language. It felt like years since I had been asked out on a date, and I was only twenty-six years old.

"I love the beach," I told him. "I always try to spend my Sundays there since I'm in class on Saturdays."

"So you're talking about a daytime date then."

The tone of Matthew's statement told me that I had committed a faux pas. I didn't care. I was more comfortable in the daytime, having reserved my nights for a twisted type of mourning where I reflected on each day and imagined my son sleeping and dreaming about me.

"All right," said Matthew. "Can I take you to the beach next Sunday?"

"I'd like that," I responded. "If we're not under a hurricane warning."

We both laughed, though our laughter was mutual acknowledgment that summertime in Florida had changed very much since our own childhoods when hurricanes were not nearly as prevalent as they had since become.

One week later, Matthew picked me up in Coral Gables and we drove to South Beach. As we cruised down U.S. 1, I learned that Matthew was also a student at FIU, studying Biomedical Engineering, specifically Orthopedic Biomechanics. Having already completed a five-year accelerated program to earn his Master's Degree, he was now a doctoral candidate about to finish his coursework. Then it was time for the real work…the dissertation. I could plainly see that he was no dummy.

As we exited Interstate 95 and got on the MacArthur Causeway to take us over to South Beach, Matthew insisted that we stop talking about him and turn our focus on me. "I want to know everything about you!" He said enthusiastically.

Like the fact that I'm still married? I don't think so. I spoke about my own studies because it was a safe topic. But Matthew kept pushing. He was trying to fill the gap between 1994 and 1997, but I wouldn't give him the satisfaction. "I spent some time overseas," I told him.

"Three years? That's nothing to shake a stick at. Where were you? And what were you doing for three years?"

"I was in Italy, teaching English."

"Wow! That sounds like an incredible experience. You must have loved it there."

I turned to Matthew and tried to express myself as kindly as possible. "I'd really rather not talk about it, if that's okay with you."

We drove to South Beach in silence as Matthew looked for a parking spot. It took almost ten minutes to accomplish that feat, which wasn't too terrible, given that it was a beautiful Sunday. As we walked along Ocean Drive and onto the white sands of the beach, Matthew finally spoke. "I'm originally from upstate New York—Syracuse—so my childhood memories of family time involve hiking in the hills. I really love the mountains. My parents relocated to Miami when Haley and I were in middle school, and I've never really taken to the beach the way I had to the mountains. So I've got to ask…What is it that you love so much about the beach?"

It was a fair question, but how could I tell him the truth? How could I tell him that I had never really loved the beach either? I had only recently come to enjoy my time here as I made it my routine to sit on the shore and let my wonderful imagination take me to Enzo. I would imagine that I could fly and that I could soar over the Atlantic and be with my son. I knew that, geographically, the first land I would hit if I flew due east was Morocco. But in my dreams, I would fly in all directions to cross the Strait of Gibraltar, soar over the Mediterranean Sea, reach the western coast of Italy, and fly over the Apennine Mountains to look down over Bologna and my little boy.

I couldn't tell Matthew about that. "I like the beach because the ocean is so vast that it reminds me of the endless possibilities in life."

It was not a dishonest answer, and Matthew seemed to like the poetry of it. He smiled as he nodded his head in understanding.

After spending too many hours in the baking sun, we decided to stroll around South Beach, so we headed up to Alton Road, where things took on a more commercial atmosphere. It was not long before we happened upon the austere monument of the Holocaust Memorial. I tried to pretend that I didn't notice it, but Matthew could not. We both stopped and observed for a moment. Then, Matthew took my hand, led me onto the grounds, and spoke softly. "As a Jew, I feel that it's always my obligation to pay my respects, even if it doesn't suit me."

As we toured the museum, I can admit that I was more shocked by the fact that Matthew was Jewish than by the images of torture projected on the walls. I had seen those photographs too many times throughout my Jewish education and sadly enough had become a bit desensitized. As I watched Matthew read every placard beneath every photo, I realized that I was committing a grave crime by feeling so hardened by the images. In honor of my new-found friend and in honor of my son, I paid attention to the horror before me with new eyes. I left the Holocaust Museum with a new appreciation for everything that I had been silently fighting for in Italy.

Matthew and I spent the rest of that great day talking about many things, none of which had to do with Italy or the Holocaust, and I found Matthew's open manner more attractive than I wanted to admit. In the weeks that followed, I spent more and more time with Matthew and his sister as the three of us would frequently meet for dinner after a full day of classes or research. But as time went on and we had become more of a trio than a couple, Matthew started demanding my Saturday nights, which was fine with me so long as he didn't intrude upon my Sunday night journal-writing ritual.

By the winter holidays, Matthew had declared his love for me. I couldn't return his words at that time, but he seemed satisfied with the fact that at least I knew how he felt.

Though I have many weaknesses, one of my greatest strengths is my ability to dedicate myself to whatever really matters at the moment. That strength, ironically, also feeds one of my weaknesses…my inability to multi-task on a big scale. I cannot put my heart into a job if I'm emotionally involved with someone, which might explain the lack of professional respect I felt in Bologna. To be fair, if I'm involved in new love, my work suffers. I was not open enough to Matthew's advances to sacrifice the bigger picture, which involved my graduation, eventual employment, financial solvency, and return to parental status. I still lived the fantasy that if I could get my American life together, then my loose strings in Italy would neatly tie themselves up.

In the spring of 1999, all of my efforts and concentration were focused on finishing my classes so that I would be ready for my summer internship and eventual graduation in August. I continued dating Matthew but was actually spending more time with Haley since we were on the same chronological path in school. While my hopes were to get a teaching position at FIU upon graduation, Haley had her heart set on returning to Syracuse. She had only attended a Florida university to take financial advantage of her residency status, but her allegiance was all New York. One day over lunch, Haley took the opportunity to do some investigation on behalf of her brother.

"So you definitely plan on staying in Miami after graduation?" She asked.

"I do."

"Would you ever consider coming to Syracuse? It's a wonderful educational town with many opportunities."

I looked at her, debating how frank I should be. "Are you telling me that an ESL professor has more opportunities in Syracuse than in Miami?"

"Not more, just different." She seemed to know that her argument was weak.

"Are you going to miss me that much? If so, stay here." I chided.

"It's not me. It's Matthew."

I pretended that our conversation wasn't turning as serious as Haley wanted it to turn. She continued. "I know that he really wants to return to Syracuse too, but he now talks about staying here because you're here."

"Really?" I tried to sound casual.

"Really. All I want to know, Millie, is if you feel as strongly for him as he feels for you, if that isn't putting you on the spot?"

"Are you kidding?" I asked. "Of course, you're putting me on the spot."

"I'm sorry, Millie, but I have to ask. If you're not into this relationship for the long haul, then Matthew should be returning to Syracuse. At this point, he doesn't have to be here. He could do his dissertation from New York and return to Florida when it's time to defend. If he were there, he'd be better able to network in the local orthopedic market."

"It sounds like you'd prefer that he go to Syracuse than be with me."

Haley bit her lower lip. "You're a very good friend, Millie. But you're distant sometimes, so nobody really knows what's going on in that wonderful mind of yours. I can see your dedication to teaching through your class presentations. I think you're a great teacher. But emotionally, I'm not sure what kind of dedication you have."

She had no idea, but how could she? She was right. I had never let her in. "You're a good friend too, Haley. That's why I can tell you that I frankly believe I should be having this discussion with Matthew instead of you." I tried to soften the harshness of my words.

Haley nodded in agreement and smiled at me. "If you were in love with my brother, you'd make a great sister-in-law."

I thought to myself, *I wish I were in love with your brother, but my heart belongs to a little Italian cloud angel.*

Days after my hear-to-heart with Haley, I was invited to spend the Passover dinner with the Crane family. I was flattered since Passover is a very important family holiday, one which I had always spent with my own family and cousins when I was growing up. When Matthew called to extend the invitation, I asked myself if Haley had suggested it to her parents with the hopes of lassoing me into the Crane family circle. I decided to accept the invitation since my rational side was telling me to be as open as possible to the world beyond my own secrets.

I had been concerned that my parents would take offense at my not spending the traditional Seder dinner with them, but they practically pushed me out the door with their approving smiles. They were elated that I was involved in a relationship that didn't involve an Italian and which did involve a Jew.

As I sat around the large dining table on that first night of the eight-day holiday, I was surrounded by six Cranes: Haley, Matthew, their parents, and two grandparents. I took notice of every detail of the Seder table, finding pleasure in observing the similarities and differences from family to family. While all Seder tables are adorned with the Seder plate, two candles, a plate for matzo, the books that recount the story of Passover (called Haggadahs), and several glasses of wine, including one for the Prophet Elijah, the variety was in the details. My family's Haggadahs were colorful, pictorial books that presented the story of Passover in a child-friendly manner. After all, the Passover story was supposed to be retold year after year so that Jews never forget the story of how the Egyptian Pharaoh had enslaved the Hebrews for generations until Moses, with the help of God, stood up to Pharaoh and led the Jews to their freedom and eventually to God's Ten Commandments. The Crane family's Haggadahs, in contrast, were less playful and more austere such that I was almost afraid to open the book that awaited me on my dinner plate for fear of hearing a harsher truth about the Jewish people's exodus from Egypt thousands of years ago.

Matthew's father led the Seder, guiding the rest of us as we took turns reading the different passages in the Haggadah. When it came time for the Four Questions, Matthew read, since he was the youngest person in attendance. The Four Questions are supposed to be read at the beginning of the Seder by the youngest child, to signify the innocence of the unknowing youth who needs to learn the story of Passover. Since Haley and Matthew were twins, each year they alternated who would play the role of the youngest child.

Matthew was seated to my left, and as he chanted the questions, I tried to imagine what it would be like to spend the rest of my Passover Seders with him, but my dreams came up short. I pictured my

Seder table and saw a child's empty chair, and the chair was crying out for Enzo to read the Four Questions. My son, Enzo, who would probably be taking his First Communion in a few short years. I visibly shuddered at the thought, and Matthew placed his right hand against my back and rubbed softly, without missing a beat as he asked in Hebrew why this night was different from all others.

The Passover meal was delicious and included the all-favorite matzo ball soup, brisket in its own gravy, and vegetables of the season. Everyone laughed a lot, as consuming the minimal four glasses of sweet grape wine required during the Seder will tend to make people do, and the mood was jovial. Still, as Mrs. Crane offered me a chocolate macaroon after dinner, I smiled at her but cried inside. I had survived last year's Seder with my sanity in tact, mostly because it had felt like the same old routine from my childhood, but this year's was proving to be a test of my desire to accept change verses my unwillingness to let bygones be bygones, as the world around me had suggested. For me, Enzo was not a bygone. He was my son, who still lived across the ocean on a continent where Jews had always been outsiders and, even once, concentration camp prisoners. Like those prisoners, I was not about to give up my hopes of some day being reunited with my family, and until that day came, Matthew Crane would always play second fiddle.

In August of 1999, two remarkable things happened. Haley and I graduated from the Master's Program, and Romy saw Enzo. The latter is undoubtedly a story worth telling.

Romy and David were already engaged to be married when David's boss sent him to Florence, Italy to survey the work of an up-and-coming contemporary artist. Romy, of course, jumped at the opportunity to join David as she had never really had the chance to see Italy as a tourist. Their trip would last for ten days so that David could tour the local galleries and hopefully arrange an interview with Piero Rossi, the painter in question. Though Romy had vowed to never play the sleuth again, it was she who volunteered to visit Bologna and try to check up on Enzo, even if she had to spy to do it.

Before Romy and David departed for Italy, I asked myself if it was worth it for me to attempt to enter the country. Two years had passed, but I had no idea how much power and influence Regina was willing to wield to keep me away. My guess was more than I could fight, and certainly more than Carlo would ever know.

A few days before her trip, my cyber-savvy sister decided to do an Internet search for Carlo Mazzini to see what would come up. Though I knew how to surf the Internet, it had never occurred to me to investigate Carlo because I had still not jumped feet first into the cyber world. I was still at the point of dipping my toe in the cold waters. Romy's search revealed that Carlo had been quite busy since my departure. He had graduated from his doctoral program and was a consultant for IBM. When Romy showed me the website, I was able to see a picture of my husband and discover that he was losing his battle with his receding hairline, despite not yet being even thirty years old.

Now that we knew where he worked, Romy was excited to resume her private eye work in Bologna, Italy. When she and David arrived in Florence, it was late August. The heat was stifling and the tourists equally so. The locals secretly prayed in their chapels for an early autumn or at least a cool front from their Swiss northern neighbors. On Romy and David's first weekday in town, Romy caught the train to Bologna while David was on the hunt for Piero Rossi.

Romy headed directly for Carlo's workplace, deciding that presenting herself in person would be more successful than a phone call. Fortunately for Romy but rather unfortunately for Carlo, the gatekeeper at the front desk was not much of a gatekeeper, and

Romy was directed with a friendly smile towards Carlo's office, whose door was partially open. Romy knocked lightly and poked her head in at the same time, hoping that the element of surprise would work in her favor. In a sing-song voice, she almost chanted. "*Buongiorno*, Carlo! It's me, Romy, your long lost sister-in-law."

Romy stepped cautiously into the office and remained just inside the doorway. Carlo didn't budge but just stared at my sister in shock. "Is she here with you this time?" No salutations, just fear emanating from behind a steel-framed desk.

"Relax. It's just me, again. May I come in?"

Carlo nodded his head and motioned to the empty chair in the corner of his office. Romy lifted the chair and carried it closer to Carlo's desk before taking a seat.

"So how are you?" She began.

"Fine, thank you. How is Millie?"

Carlo's question surprised Romy. "Do you really want to know, or are you just being polite?"

"I'd really like to know."

"Well," Romy hestitated. Truth or fiction? She was not sure which way to go but eventually settled on the partial truth. "She's miserable, Carlo. She's trying to get her life in order, but a very significant piece is missing...her son!"

Romy practically yelled the last phrase, and Carlo jumped up to close the door. He quickly returned to his chair and slumped down into it with an air of exhaustion. "I'm sorry that she's so miserable, but you certainly haven't traveled this far just to let me know that, now have you? Why exactly are you here?"

"I happen to be staying in Florence with my fiancé, who is doing business there, but while I'm here, I would like to see Enzo so that I can give Millie a nice report on her son. Will that be possible, or are you going to make this difficult?"

"There is no way that you will speak with my son. He thinks his mother abandoned him, which is true, and I don't want him confused."

"You mean that you don't want him to know the nasty truth about his father and grandmother." Romy was feeling feisty and quite in control.

"Truth is a relative term."

"Carlo, if you properly understood English, you would realize that it actually is not a relative term. Truth is absolute until it is manipulated by man."

"And by woman, let's not forget."

Their banter was titillating to Carlo but disturbing to Romy. "I want to see my nephew. Where can I find him, please?"

Carlo leaned back in his chair and tucked both hands behind his head, stretching his elbows out wide. "Fine. You can see him from a distance, but if you approach him or try to communicate with him in any way, he will certainly tell me about it. That's the kind of child he is. He knows not to talk to strangers."

"So where can I find him?"

Carlo surveyed Romy one last time, letting his eyes check her out from head to toe before he answered. "You're very pretty, you know?"

Romy stood up, grabbed a loose piece of paper from atop Carlo's desk, found a pen as well, and assumed the note taking stance. She looked him directly in the eye and waited. Carlo exhaled loudly. "At four o'clock this afternoon, his nanny will take him to Giardini Margherita for a gelato and some play time. If you can find him, that is, if you can recognize him, then you can see him, but I forbid you from stopping by my apartment!"

"Thank you!" Romy shouted as she left Carlo's office.

Giardini Margherita was a huge park just beyond the city walls, and at that time of day, there would be people everywhere. My sister realized that she had her work cut out for her. But Carlo was not as clever as he had thought, because Romy had fresh directions to Regina's place and my precious photo of Enzo at twenty months old to remind her of his face. Sure, he would be four years old by now with much more hair, but the photo was something.

At 3:30 in the afternoon, Romy planted herself near a column beneath the portico of Via Castiglione and waited. It was a long wait, but at 4:15, an attractive young woman, about twenty-years old, and a small boy, who looked to be about four, exited the building and turned up the street to head toward the Viale, the circular road surrounding the old city and leading to the park. The child's light brown waves and almond-shaped eyes assured Romy that she was looking at none other than her nephew, Enzo Mazzini, and she fell into step a safe distance behind him and his nanny. Romy could hear the two chatting as they walked, but the noise of the traffic compiled with the language barrier made it impossible for her to understand. As they approached the Viale and waited to cross, Romy felt safe enough to join the crowd at the crosswalk. She stood so close behind Enzo that she could have touched him, but she didn't. Instead, she exhaled one strong breath over his wavy locks. They quivered as if touched by a soft breeze, and Romy felt satisfied that she had sent some positive energy Enzo's way.

Once inside the park, Enzo and the nanny headed directly to the gelato stand. Romy fell in line about two people behind and was so excited to be able to learn Enzo's favorite flavor of ice cream. It was *nocciola*, which is hazelnut. She practiced saying the word a thousand times in her head so she wouldn't forget it when she returned to Miami; she wanted to be able to bring me something from my son.

With gelato in hand, Enzo and the nanny headed towards a park bench. The nanny sat down and immediately popped open her cell phone. It became glued to her ear, which bothered Romy on the one hand because the nanny should have been giving undivided attention to Enzo, but pleased Romy as well. It meant that she might have the chance to approach Enzo unnoticed. As soon as the thought struck Romy, Enzo darted off to the water fountain, which was easily twenty yards from the nanny's bench. Romy casually arose from her own bench farther down the path and walked towards Enzo. She stood right behind him, pretending to wait for the water fountain.

"Is the water cold?" Romy asked Enzo.

He looked over his shoulder in surprise but responded in perfect English. "It's really cold. It hurts my teeth." He continued drinking.

"Where did you learn English?"

"I don't know. TV and my nanny, I guess. I just know it."

Enzo took one last sip and turned to leave, but Romy stopped him. "Are you Enzo?" She braved to ask.

"How do you know my name? You're a stranger." Enzo took a step back.

"It's okay, Enzo." Romy realized that identifying herself would probably traumatize the boy, so she chose to be vague. And she didn't care one iota if Enzo reported anything back to his father. "I'm not a total stranger. I knew you when you were a baby, about two years old. I haven't seen you since then. You've really grown so well. You're so big and strong." She smiled warmly at him, and he couldn't help but smile back.

"I have to go now," he said. As he ran away, he shouted, "It was nice meeting you!"

Romy was very pleased with the encounter and chose to stick around for a bit longer. She kept her distance and waited until Enzo had involved himself in a solitary game of kick with a stray soccer ball. Romy pulled out her camera and set it on telephoto, which is how I came to have my fourth and most recent picture of my son. I can't see his features very well, but I know that it's him and I know that he's happy.

Romy and David got married in November. It was a beautiful Jewish ceremony in a beautiful historic synagogue, and I, of course, was the Maid of Honor, a title that the family had debated using since I was, in reality, the Matron of Honor. It was decided that my life was not being conducted under the laws of matrimony and that it was no one's business but ours. It was as if I were a born-again virgin.

I have to admit that it was very hard for me to stand so close to my dear sister and watch her have the type of wedding which I had always dreamed about. I was happy for her but feeling quite sorry for myself, and I thought of the old song by Smoky Robinson, *Tears of a Clown*. That was me as I helped bless the sanctity of my sister and brother-in-law's union with a smile on my face and then ran back to the bride's dressing room to cry for all my sins.

As 2000 drew nearer, I found myself quite comfortable in my new role as an ESL Instructor at FIU's English Language Institute. The campus was so familiar to me that it had become my home away from home. I felt youthful being in a college environment where young, hopeful faces constantly reminded me that the possibilities were endless. I was twenty-seven years old, and the world was my oyster. Despite my professional satisfaction, I had come to believe two sad facts: I was not in love with Matthew Crane, and I had to find a way to get divorced. They might seem like unrelated ideas, but I believe that part of the reason why Matthew never got the best of me was because I was tied to Carlo. I wasn't in love with my husband. Lord knows that those feelings had long gone, but through Enzo, my connection with Carlo would be eternal. Too much lack of trust had already surfaced between Matthew and me, and I believed that relationship to be doomed. Ironically, it was that sense of doom that made me realize that I had to find a way to break my legal obligations to Carlo, else end up a very lonely woman.

I contacted a divorce attorney and discovered that I was eligible for a petition for dissolution of marriage simply by residing in Florida for more than six months. To make matters easier, Florida was a no-fault state, which meant that I could just file with the courthouse without having to prove any due cause. The catch was that I had to notify Carlo by mailing him a waiver, which he would have to sign and return.

What if he wouldn't agree? What if he had some motive for keeping me legally obligated to him? I couldn't imagine that scenario because he would then be limiting his own future as well, so I decided to take action and began the petition process. I expected to have Carlo's response within three weeks, allowing for round trip postal service and some days in between for Carlo to dwell over the papers before signing. With Christmas soon approaching, I thought that Carlo would appreciate the gift of freedom.

You can therefore imagine my surprise when just two days after sending out my papers to Carlo, my mother called with very strange news. "Millie, you'll never in a million years guess who has sent you a package to my address…Carlo!"

It was all I could do not to drop the receiver. "Open it. Tell me what's inside."

My mother opened the manila envelope. It was Carlo's first correspondence in more than two years. "There's a note." She paused to read. "He wishes you well and says that Enzo is doing great." She paused some more, but her voice had changed when she continued speaking. "He's asking you to sign the enclosed papers. He's requesting an annulment."

Within twenty minutes, I was seated at my mother's kitchen table. I perused the papers, whose Italian legalese made it very hard to understand, which is surely why Carlo had spelled it out for me in his note. My heart sank to realize how differently our minds worked but how in sync they were…different means to the same end. But an annulment was quite different from a divorce. An annulment was saying that the marriage never existed, that the child born to the couple was illegitimate, and that it was all a farce. I knew that the divorce process in Italy worked quite differently from the American process and that it could keep a person in marital limbo for up to five years, but why would Carlo risk stigmatizing our son? Then it hit me. He wants to remarry…soon. I would have had a bit of power in my hands if I hadn't already mailed out my own request for divorce. But Carlo didn't want a Florida divorce; he wanted to be recognized as eligible to marry in Italy. I wondered if we both could have what we legally wanted, but then I stopped myself. His petition for annulment had been filed long before my petition for divorce.

By the time I returned to my apartment, it was three o'clock in the afternoon. I picked up the phone and called Italy. Carlo answered the phone, probably not having considered screening his calls since it wasn't the weekend.

"*Ciao*, Carlo."

I didn't have to identify myself. "Millie! My God! How are you?"

"I'm fine. How's Enzo?" I pleaded for some information with one simple question.

"He's great. Big. Really smart. You're sister spoke to him last summer, but I'm sure you know that."

I nodded my head but couldn't speak because I was holding tears in my throat.

"So I guess you got my package," Carlo said.

I swallowed hard and was able to speak. "Yes. The funny thing is that you should be receiving a package from me in a few days…requesting a divorce."

"Are you kidding me? Are you trying to get married too?"

There it was—a confession.

"Not at all. I just want my life back."

"Well, Millie, you know that divorce in Italy takes a very long time. That's why I went for the annulment."

"I figured as much. Why else would you bastardize your son?"

"That's very cruel, Millie, but I won't fight back because I know that in some ways, I've wronged you."

In some ways? I screamed inside my head, but my brain would not let my lips part. They were pressed together too tightly. I forced myself to breathe deeply and was then able to open my mouth. "So here's the thing, Carlo. I'll sign your annulment papers if you'll sign my divorce papers. That will make the divorce valid in Florida so that I can acknowledge with pride that I have a son through what was once a legitimate marriage, and you can have your annulment, clean and easy."

"But that's like...what do you call it? Double jeopardy. I'll have to have my signature on your papers notarized which will prove I'm getting divorced in one place and annulled in another."

I had no tolerance for his problems. "Your mother seems to have influence. I'm sure she can work it out. In fact, I will not mail back your papers until I've received my own, properly signed."

"And why should you get yours first?"

Carlo was up for the fight, but I was prepared to shoot from the hip. "Because *you* have our son."

As the winter holidays approached with all the fanfare that the end of the millennium had promised, Matthew was feeling restless. I assumed that he was anxious to see his sister, who had left for Syracuse four months earlier but would be returning within a few weeks for the holidays. I was certainly excited to see my old friend, but I sensed that Matthew had something other than his sister's visit brewing in his mind.

One early December Sunday, Matthew met me at Romy and David's place on South Beach. I had slept there the night before, claiming that I needed some alone time. Matthew was disappointed that I had chosen date night to want my alone time, but he didn't falter in booking me for Sunday. Winters on the beach were my favorite time. I would dress in jeans and a light blouse and sit out on the sand for hours watching the fair-skinned tourists wade in the ocean and shun the use of sun block, damaging their skin beyond repair. Matthew sat with me on that particular Sunday, and we both gazed out at the horizon in silence.

"What would you like for Chanukah?" Matthew asked.

Enzo, was the first thought that came to my mind, but instead I said, "Nothing really."

"Well, you're no help." Matthew lightly elbowed my ribs, causing me to pull away from the tickling sensation. Then he changed the topic. "I have a different question."

"Okay."

"For the new year and the new millennium, would you please give some thought to the idea of what you want for your future with me?" Without doubt, Matthew was bold, but it was hard to fault him for his straight shooting. "I love you, Millie."

I felt ready to share a little piece of myself with my boyfriend as I silently flew across the Atlantic to visit my past. "I know. Thank you, Matthew, but I'm not sure I deserve your love."

"What kind of self-deprecating complex have you got? Why aren't you worthy of my love?"

"Because I've been lying to you about something very important."

"Why would anyone lie about something that didn't matter?"

It was a strange response that I chose to ignore as I continued. "Back in Italy, I was married."

"I figured it was something like that," he responded.

"But I'm actually still married, Matthew. I'm working on getting divorced, but I've been lying to you."

"Why did you lie? Did you think I wouldn't like you if I knew?"

"I wasn't ready to talk about it."

"For over a year, you weren't ready to talk about it?" He was clearly frustrated. "I guess you don't feel that close to me." Now, he sounded hurt.

"It's not that, Matthew. It's a big deal, you know."

"Why have you waited so long to try to end the marriage? Were you hoping for reconciliation?" Matthew sounded very concerned.

"Kind of, but not the kind of reconciliation you're thinking of."

"Damn it, Millie! You're talking in code. Please talk straight with me!"

"The truth is too messy. You don't really want to be involved." I turned to look back out over the water, but Matthew would have none of it.

"I want to marry you, for God's sake! Nothing could be that messy, Millie! Life is not as complex as you make it out to be. It's all a big drama with you!"

I looked Matthew directly in the eye but could barely see him through my own tears. "I have a son, Matthew…a son who I haven't seen since 1997, one day after he turned two years old." I stood up and yelled at Matthew through clenched teeth. "I have been prohibited from ever seeing him again, and it has killed me inside. That is my drama, and that is why there's no room for me to love you!"

I ran away as fast as the thick sand would allow me to run. It was probably a very awkward scene, but as soon as my feet hit pavement, I was history. If Matthew was trying to chase me down, I never knew it because before I realized it, I had reached Romy's apartment, about eight large blocks from the beach. I leaned against the front door, at first hyperventilating and then panting until I could get my breathing under control. The residential street was quiet. The only noise was the rustling of trees and an occasional car passing by. Eventually, even the sound of my own breathing became indiscernible. I entered the quiet apartment and fell asleep.

I did not see my friend Haley that holiday season. It was all too awkward to deal with and easy enough to avoid. On her last night in town, however, Haley phoned me and found me alone in my apartment.

"I know this has been a rough time for you," she began.

"I'm sorry, Haley. I really would have loved to see you, but when I have problems with Matthew, I have problems with your family."

"Millie, how many other close friends do you have? I mean friends who you consider intimate…people you can count on?"

"Just you, Haley." I practically whispered my response.

"So that means that you have no one in the world to tell your secrets to," Haley poignantly stated.

"I have Romy."

"But now she has David."

"Haley, I didn't want to share my past with Matthew, and you were too close to him. How could I share with you and not expect it to influence my relationship with your brother?"

Haley's tone changed as she spoke again. "I consider you a good friend, Millie, but I don't think I've ever completely trusted you. I've always sensed that you were hiding something, which is why I never opened up to you either."

"You're turning the tables on me, Haley. You want me to feel guilty for not confiding in you." I said it matter-of-factly but without anger.

"I did it a long time ago, Millie. But I'll fess up now if you can promise me that there will always be trust between us."

The conversation was moving in a direction that I hadn't anticipated. "So even if Matthew and I aren't together anymore, you feel comfortable being my friend?"

"Are you willing to withhold judging my secret?"

"Who am I to judge?"

There was a brief silence before Haley spoke again. "When I was growing up, my parents used to say that I had a dark side. I guess it was the way I expressed myself or explained my perception of things. I never really understood what they meant, but in high school, I became their self-fulfilling prophecy when I became addicted to cocaine. I'd been using it here and there since middle school, but it didn't get out of control until high school. I never got caught with drugs, but I did get arrested for shoplifting black eyeliner. Can you believe it? Black eyeliner, so I could show my dark side." She laughed at the thought. "There's always some way that druggies manage to destroy their luck, and I think, deep down, I wanted to get caught. Anyway, my parents eventually put me into a rehab center, which caused me to be held back in eleventh grade, mostly because I ended up on the extended-stay program when I was caught screwing another patient in the hospital. I don't even remember his name." Haley paused as if trying to pull the boy's name from the deepest recesses of her memory. "Whatever. It was a rough time followed by years of psychotherapy before I had any friends again, but I've stayed clean. And I made a friend. So why don't you and I solidify that friendship by beginning with you telling me your whole story."

Our phone call lasted for hours that night, and when we hung up, I cried because I had wasted so much time closing myself off from people like Haley, Matthew, and who knows how many others. I felt old and worn out, and I wanted to feel young again.

As the calendar rolled into 2000, I watched the apple drop in New York City and wondered how Dick Clark had preserved his youth so miraculously. I watched the revelry in Times Square and realized that I had South Beach. Date night was not an option for me anymore since Matthew had not yet tried to win me back, and so my Saturday evenings turned into nights of wild parties at various South Beach dance clubs that lasted until sunrise. It's amazing how easy it is to make friends when your mind is open and your veins are full of alcohol. For the first time in my life, I had a social life. I didn't date as much as experiment with casual sex and the independence of making my own choices. It was so much easier when love wasn't on the line, though I must mention that I always used protection. There was not enough alcohol in the world to make me forget the consequences of not doing so.

Speaking of consequences, it was in early February when I finally received the signed waiver from Carlo. I returned to the courthouse to appear before a judge, who divorced me then and there, just days after my fifth wedding anniversary. It was a Friday, and so I immediately kept my end of the bargain by signing and posting the annulment papers before the end of the business day. I then chose to celebrate by hitting my new-found stomping grounds on Ocean Drive in South Beach and waking up the following morning with a painful hangover.

Romy and David were not fond of my new lifestyle, and I believe that they wanted to evict me from their apartment on Sundays. But my sister knows me better than I know myself, and she had the patience to hold out a few more months for the end of this phase in my life, which brings me to Enzo's fifth birthday.

As I sat there looking out at the tight bodies and hungover faces of my contemporaries, I was sobered by the thought that my son was turning five years old and in one day I would be twenty-eight. I missed Enzo so badly that I could feel my stomach tighten up and turn over. That clean slate that I had so looked forward to at the turn of the millennium had been grossly abused, and I knew it. I wanted a change, and I even found myself thinking more and more of Matthew. Haley had recently reported that Matthew had moved up to Syracuse to do research at the university. She said that he was happy with his work but constantly asked her about me, which left me wondering why he had never asked *me* about me. It was not his nature to be afraid of getting what he wanted, but perhaps it was his nature to spite. The truth was that I really didn't know him all that well because I had never given myself the chance.

On Sunday evening, July second, I pulled out my journal as I did every Sunday night, and I began to write to Enzo.

My dear Enzo,

Yesterday was your fifth birthday and today is my twenty-eighth. The years are flying, and I feel farther away from you than ever. While I was at the beach this weekend, I flew across the ocean to see you at your birthday party. Of course, it was all in my imagination, and I envisioned a beautiful party for you with balloons, cake, and lots of your friends. I hope you have friends who are good to you. Kids can be cruel sometimes, but a true friend is a wonderful gift. I've just recently found my true friend, but she lives so far away and I miss her very much. But not nearly as much as I miss you!

I still dream that some day, somehow, I will be able to see you and show you this journal that I've been keeping since 1997. I hope you'll begin to understand how much I wanted to be in your life and how you've been in my thoughts every single day of my life. Until that day comes, I wish you a very Happy Birthday, my love. Good night for now. Sogni d'oro…sweet dreams!

Love, Your forever mamma

CHAPTER 2

▼

Like I said, I'm a Syracuse boy. And since I returned, I've seen what they mean when they say you can never go back. I've got a great career, a great apartment, and even the kind of girlfriend I thought I always wanted, but this place is no childhood paradise. Then again, I suppose nowhere in the world is a childhood paradise once childhood slips away.

Back in Miami, I was right when I said that someone was going to happen to me, and boy, did she ever happen to me. From the moment I first saw Millie, she slammed me against the wall with her innocent vulnerability and her guarded ways. Before I knew it, I was pinned there with nowhere to go except into her arms because a man's got to admit when he figures himself out. And I'm an explorer, which means I'm the kind of man who can't resist a woman like Millie, the kind of woman whose maps can't be easily charted, whose heart is closed but begging to be opened, whose sexuality explodes in private, like some hidden evil twin. Oh, yeah. Millie Gossett is a vixen in the bedroom, though I'm sure her side of the story never goes there because that's not her aim. She is so focused on her big secrets and her role as the beautiful martyr that she can't see beyond her own nose. But I was telling you about Millie's passionate side because that's the part of her that captured me and let me know that she had love deep within her and the strongest desire I've ever seen to be loved back.

I suffer from the Camilla Complex, which is the name of my self-diagnosed tendency to be attracted like a magnet to dramatic women who indulge in self-pity. It all started when I was in tenth grade and had my first serious girlfriend—Camilla Capriati. She was funny, daring, and strikingly beautiful. Her father was the dean of the foreign language department at the University of Miami and an active member of the Catholic community. When he found out that Camilla was dating a Jewish boy (dare he not think about the chance of her falling in love with one!), Camilla was virtually forbidden to see me. *Your mother and I strongly recommend that you stop seeing that boy immediately since it will only lead to no good,* were Dean Capriati's actual words. This, of course, only made me more attractive to Camilla and her more enticing to me as the forbidden fruit. But she played the martyr well, and she eventually broke my heart, claiming that our love was doomed, like Romeo and Juliet, and that she would always remember me as her first love. I think Camilla was more in love with the romantic tragedy aspect of our relationship than with me, but I still look at her as the one who set the mold for the kind of woman I would end up always pursuing...the understated drama queen.

Even though Millie is a cliché for me, I did love her! Lord, I would have married her if she'd given me the chance. That day on the beach when she finally spoke about her son, I would have listened. I wouldn't have thrown her away like some used person because, damn it, she was the goods...for me, at least. But she ran away like a child, and I suppose I did the same by trying to come home…to a place where my childhood no longer exists.

They were good times with Millie in Miami. My sister, my girlfriend, and I…a strange triangle of love and friendship. But Millie was good for Haley. Still is, I imagine, though Haley is also here in Syracuse now, so I don't know what goes on in their friendship. I've tried to move on, forget Millie, but the truth is that I hear myself often asking about her when I least expect to, when Haley hasn't even been talking about her, when I'm caught in the world of wishing I were back in Florida with Millie. So there you have it. You can see that I'm a hard man to please. When I lived in Florida, all I bitched about was getting back to Syracuse. And now that I'm back here, all I bitch about is missing my time with Millie in Florida. That's what makes me think that places are only as important as the memories we make there, meaning that if my childhood had sucked in Syracuse, I would see this town as barren tundra, a wasteland. By the same token, if I had grown up in Miami, my childhood nostalgia would reek of sand and seashells, moss and swamp. The truth is that home is where love lies, and from what Haley has told me, Millie's home is in Italy. That's where her boy is.

So I go through my days trying not to think about my tortured soul of an ex-girlfriend and focus my energies on reliving the glory days of my childhood. When I'm not working, I'm hiking, usually with my present girlfriend who loves the outdoors of upstate New York as much as I do. She's carefree and independent and honest…basically an open book, which (as I said before) goes against my explorer nature. She's good in bed, but that's no surprise. She's super athletic and fun to be with outdoors, so why wouldn't she be so indoors? Which brings me back to my point; there's no element of surprise. Believe it or not, when Millie broke her news to me about her hidden child, the shock stimulated me. Crazy? Reckless? Perhaps, but it's me. Millie's the kind of girl who I firmly believe will never run out of surprises because, even when life takes on the predictable rhythm of every day living, Millie will never be predictable. She's too caught up in her self-analysis to settle for status quo. If she hadn't run away from me, I know I could have been happy with her. So why didn't I chase her? Because as much as I love exploring and discovering, I want to be explored too, and if Millie would only express the desire to discover me…Well, I won't hold my breath. Millie won't venture out on such an expedition. I'm not sure if she ever has.

For Labor Day weekend, I decided to take my first vacation since returning to the States in 1997. I flew to Syracuse to visit Haley, knowing very well that there was a strong chance I would have to face Matthew, but he had been on my mind the more I stayed away from the clubs and the less I punished myself for my past. Apart from not pursuing me when I left him on the beach, Matthew had never faltered in his ways. He was consistent and, I had come to realize, trustworthy. He came from a good family who supported each other under the worst of circumstances and who celebrated each other's successes. This I knew because Haley had notified me of Matthew's successful doctoral defense just one week prior to the Labor Day holiday. He had returned to Miami for the event, which led me to wonder why he hadn't tried to call me. Then I wizened up and realized that he was dealing with the most important event in his career to date, and messing with his past was not on the agenda.

Anyway, he knew that I would be in Syracuse one week later, and I was hoping that he would be open to contact at that time.

I flew into Syracuse on a blustery Friday evening. The captain had mentioned that the weather was unseasonably cold for the city, but I doubted that. I figured he said that to all the visitors, too ashamed to admit that people lived in a place that was so frigid in early September, dare we even think about wintertime. Haley greeted me at the airport with a hug warm enough to make me forget the climate. It had been just over a year since we had last seen each other.

We went out to a late dinner and hugged our coffee mugs with both hands as we chatted in a cozy pub with a lit fireplace. Even our server commented on the unexpected weather in an attempt to justify the burning fire. Haley and I chatted and chatted until she finally commented on how much I had changed.

"You're a brighter person since I last saw you. It's like you've found life again. Have you been keeping another secret from me? Are you in love?"

She smiled coyly as she asked the question, and I thought carefully before I answered. "No more secrets here and no new love, either. I've just been looking at things differently since my last birthday, and I have to admit that I've been thinking an awful lot about your handsome brother."

Haley put down her coffee mug, breaking my eye contact as she did so. "I've got to tell you, Millie. Matthew's been dating someone. I don't think it's so serious yet, but he's moving on. He likes it here, and the girl he's dating loves hiking. He thinks he's hit the jackpot."

I would be lying if I said that I wasn't disappointed, but I asked Haley anyway if she thought that Matthew would be willing to see me. She didn't answer but just handed me her cell phone and told me to press number two, Matthew's speed dial code. I took the phone nervously and followed her instructions. When I heard Matthew's voice on the line, my heart beat in double time.

"Hi, Matthew. It's Millie."

"Well hello, Stranger." His voice was pleasant and non-threatening.

"I'm sitting in a pub with your sister right now."

"I know," he said. "Her number came up on my caller ID."

I smiled and tried to be bold. "Would you be willing to see me, Matthew?" I closed my eyes and clenched my teeth, awaiting his response.

"Of course. I've been waiting for your call."

"Haley told you that I would call you?" I was angry.

"I mean since last December."

Now, I was silenced.

Then Matthew made a proposal. "How about breakfast tomorrow morning…I'll pick you up at Haley's at nine."

The preparation for a long-awaited reunion is always full of yin and yang. There's the excitement of anticipated pleasure at seeing the person from your past mixed with the feelings of anxiety when you remember what it was about the past that separated you in the first place. There's the hope of better things to come as you prepare for your fantasy encounter mixed with the fear that your dreams will crumble when the encounter proves to be all too human. You try to look your best and do everything in your power to make it so, yet your heart races and your body overreacts. This makes you look anything but your best when clammy skin and an unnatural, ruddy complexion reveal that you're not exactly calm and collected. Everything feels out of balance, but in reality it's the perfect balance of yin and yang.

At nine o'clock sharp the next morning, Matthew rang Haley's doorbell. She had decided to sleep in since I was heading out, so I tiptoed through the apartment to greet the man who used to want to marry me.

When I opened the door and saw Matthew for the first time in nine months, it hit me like a ton of bricks. I saw my life from the summer of 1998 until the winter of 1999 pass before my eyes like the old Super-eight films from my youth. There was now enough time behind me that I could see the little things that I had missed when I was experiencing them…Matthew's half-crooked smile, his sharp wit, his unquestionable devotion. I couldn't love him then because I wouldn't allow myself the freedom to do so. I felt a moment of remorse as I thought back to my reckless nights of the earlier part of the year, but I quickly forgave myself and hoped that Matthew would forgive me for the truth that had emerged on the beach last December.

Matthew looked down at my boots and then smiled sincerely. "I see you don't have your running shoes on, so it's a good start."

"It's good to see you, Matthew," I responded.

He leaned forward and kissed me on the cheek. "Before you step out of the apartment and this goes any further, I want you to know that I've already chosen our topic of discussion for this breakfast meeting."

His tone was serious, and I was taken aback. "All right…" I hesitated.

"I want to know all about your son."

Once the truth was on the table, it didn't look quite as messy as I had thought it would. Matthew had listened to my story without interruption but with the encouraging *uh-huh's* and *hmm's* necessary to prove his focus, and when I finished speaking, he smiled at me. "Did you know that my mother and father are second cousins?"

My expression went blank. I didn't know what that had to do with anything or what he was getting at.

"My point is," he clarified, "That most families have some strange secret they keep locked in a closet."

"Do you cry when you think about your parents being related?" I asked.

"No."

"Then it isn't really the same kind of secret, now is it?"

Matthew reached across the table to hold my right hand. "I'm sorry. I didn't mean to minimize your pain. I'm just trying to say that it's not something that should have come between us."

"But it did." I was nodding my head. "And now you have a girlfriend, who I hear is great."

"Yeah." Matthew was nodding back. "But my confession for the morning is that I still carry a torch for you, Millie."

I couldn't hide the smile that was spreading across my face. "So now what?" I asked with trepidation.

"We stay in touch, visit when we can, and see where time takes us."

My smile faded.

"Millie, I can't just pack up again and move back to Miami. I've got a career starting here, and I like it here. Let's just see how things go."

It was such a man's answer, but I had to respect it.

I turn on the shower and stick my hand under the running water until it is just the right temperature. I step onto the shower's blue ceramic floor and suddenly hear a child crying. "Shaya wif me, Mamma! Shaya wif me!" I look over my shoulder and see a small boy covered in soap suds, but he is suspended just inches above the ground. I realize that he is an angel with puffy white wings fluttering behind him. "Buongiorno, Cloud Angel," I say, but he is rising higher and higher into the sky, floating away from me as he cries, "Shaya wif me, Mamma!"

I woke up in the middle of the night from the sound of my own sobbing. I had had the dream that used to haunt me when I first returned to the States, but which hadn't visited me in a very long time. I sat up in bed and took deep breaths, trying to understand why the dream had returned to me now. I looked at the clock. It was only minutes after midnight on that almost Tuesday morning, so in Italy it was six o'clock in the morning. Maybe, on some deep subconscious level, Enzo had been dreaming about me or dreaming about our shower together, and that's why I dreamed it too. Even though it was highly unlikely that my theory could hold a drop of water, I liked the idea, and I closed my eyes tightly, trying to send my energy out to Enzo in case he was receptive.

It was November of 2000, more than three years since I had seen my son, and I had done an admirable job of moving on with my life, as I had been so instructed. But no matter how many years had distanced me from the trauma of losing Enzo, no matter how well my career was going (and it was going very well), no matter how sweet things had recently been in my love life, my heart ached at one moment or another every day of my life. I thought about women who give up their babies for adoption and how difficult it must be for some of them, but I couldn't completely relate. Their decisions may have eventually been regretted or not, but at least they could look in the mirror and say that they had made a choice and that they were the masters of their fates. I had never been given the choice, and I had not found the ability to look at my loss and find the positive. That was when I started actively praying for the demise of Regina Buonsignore. I had accepted that Carlo was a weak man and that as long as his mamma was alive, I had no chance of gaining access to Enzo. I knew that I didn't have the courage to engage in foul play, but I hoped that between my prayers and Regina's bad karma, I might get lucky.

Thanksgiving was approaching, which gave me something to look forward to. Matthew would be coming to Miami, and it would be our first visit since my Labor Day visit to New York. We had been chatting regularly since then, talking about everything from the mundane to the intimate. It was a very different kind of relationship than the one we had shared for sixteen months when Matthew had been local. This time it was more open and more honest. I was very excited to see him, especially since he had informed me in our last phone conversation that he had finally stopped seeing "the hiking chick," as I had so unaffectionately called her.

In my earlier story telling of Matthew and me, I never mentioned the first time that we had made love or any times after that, mostly because it wasn't the most significant part of our relationship…at that time. Now, however, things were very different. Matthew stayed at my apartment on the Friday night after Thanksgiving, and we made love. Although it was far from our first time, it was certainly the first time in a very long time and the first time that I had given myself completely to him. I felt relaxed, which wasn't my typical nature during moments of intimacy, and I allowed myself to receive pleasure on a higher level, much in the same way that I had only given it in the past. Unfortunately, I cannot say for sure if Matthew felt as giving as I did. Perhaps my new behavior surprised him, and although many men like surprises in bed, some are actually so thrown off by them that the moment is lost. The tables had turned and Matthew had become the guarded soul. I tried to cut him some slack, admitting that if he vacillated at all, it was my fault. Coming back into a relationship after any hiatus involves a change in dynamic, whether a couple wants to face it or not. For Matthew and me, life had happened and things had changed. It would take time for us to adapt, and I was patient enough to go the distance. As for Matthew, I couldn't say.

The day after renewing our love affair, I told Matthew something that I had never told him before as the two of us sat on the beach and pretended to fly to Italy.

"I love you, Matthew." It felt so good to say that I didn't even care if he said it back or not, which was a good thing because he did not.

Matthew just looked at me and said, "Some day, I'd like to fly to Italy with you, for real."

His response was okay with me. *Some day* implied a time in the future, which implied that he could imagine a future with me, and I was willing to take what I could get.

By early 2001, I thought that things were going rather well in my life. I had mastered the ability to make it through a whole week sometimes without breaking into tears. But then Celine Dion's son was born. Her fans had been well aware of the famous singer's mixed tale of a blessed life hit by bouts of tragedy, and so when her first child, Renee Charles, was born, she released a song in his honor. *A New Day Has Come* became an instant hit and therefore received heavy air play on all the pop music and easy listening radio stations, but for me, it was a nightmare. Her song broke down all my barriers and brought me to tears by something as simple as its melody, not to speak of the lyrics. While Celine and her husband celebrated their new gift, I reverted to daydreams of my twenty-fifth birthday and my little cloud angel.

I shared my torment with Matthew, who tried his best to be sympathetic, but the truth is that without being a parent, it is difficult for anyone to truly empathize with the loss of a child. As 2001 progressed, I felt that my talk of Enzo was pushing Matthew and me apart instead of bringing us together. Yes, he wanted to know about my son and my pain but only in small doses. Unfortunately for us, my pain did not measure itself out so sparingly.

I visited Matthew in March, when FIU went on its Spring Break, and he visited over Memorial Day weekend. I visited for Independence Day, arriving on the afternoon of the third since I wouldn't dare miss sharing my birthday with Enzo. I kept my ocean date with my son and flew off to Syracuse the next day.

The July Fourth festivities were like none I'd ever experienced. Matthew and Haley took me to Longbranch Park in Liverpool, a suburb on the north end of Onondaga Lake. We gathered with the crowds, setting up our picnic blankets on the hillside so we could look down on the amphitheater with the beautiful Seneca River behind it. From the bandstand, the Syracuse Symphony's performance of patriotic marches began at dusk and continued until dark. At that time, the orchestra's closing number was Tchaikovsky's *1812 Overture*, the music coinciding with the shooting of an old cannon, whose ammunition headed into the river. The cannon's final shot signaled the commencement of the fireworks display over the Seneca, whose river banks were graced by old Weeping Willows and purple irises.

I was so far from Miami, and it felt good. I even asked myself if I could live in a place as idyllic as this, but by the time Matthew visited me for Labor Day, I realized that a full year had passed since our reunion and the recommencement of our dating; I was not sure that our relationship was going anywhere.

The weekend following Matthew's Labor Day visit, he had informed me that he would be in New York City for an orthopedics seminar. I had no idea of the exact dates of the conference, so when I woke up on September 11, 2001, I didn't know if my boyfriend was in New York City or Syracuse. As the morning's tragic events unfolded on live television, I sat frozen like the rest of America, worrying about my loved one. I tried calling Matthew's cell phone, but the circuits were always busy. I finally reached Haley's voice mail and left a teary message that begged her to call me as soon as possible. Then it occurred to me to call his parents here in Miami, but like me, they didn't know the dates of his stay in the city and had been going through their own private hell.

At 11:35 in the morning on that terrible Tuesday, Matthew called me...from New York City. He was safe. His conference had been at the Waldorf Astoria Hotel, safely far enough away from Ground Zero but close enough to see the black clouds looming above the city and to smell the acrid odor of all that was burning. As I cried in relief to hear his voice over the phone, he described the scenes in the city, and my tears of joy turned to those of mourning.

As Matthew continued reporting on the morning's events, I interrupted him. "Have you called your parents or Haley yet?" I completely expected him to say yes.

"No, I wanted to call you first so you wouldn't worry."

"Are you crazy?" I almost shouted at him.

"I just didn't want you to think for even one minute that you'd lost Enzo and me, too."

What could I say? Any doubts that I had secretly kept about Matthew's devotion to me were quickly erased, and I voiced my admiration. "I love you, Matthew."

"I love you too, Millie."

When a couple becomes so comfortable in a long distance relationship, it's hard for them to make the move from frequent flyers to twenty-four/seven partners. Matthew and I had certainly come to be complacent about our relationship, but don't doubt for a moment that we loved each other; we definitely did. The problem was that we also loved our careers in our respective cities such that discussion of one of us relocating to be closer to the other managed to fall by the wayside...for two more years.

When Matthew brought up the idea for the first time of my relocating to Syracuse, I had just earned tenure at the university. You didn't have to be in the world of academia to grasp the importance and value of my circumstance, and Matthew did. So I reached for the proverbial brass ring and suggested that he return to Miami, to which he replied that he had never liked it there and thought he would be miserable. If he had been a Billy Joel fan, I would have quoted him the lyrics, *Whenever we're together, that's my home,* hoping to inspire him. I told Matthew that I was starting to feel that I wasn't enough for him, and he started to realize that maybe I was right. By Christmas of 2003, Matthew and I had broken up...again.

CHAPTER 3

▼

Do you know what happens when things get comfortable? Life gets scary. Comfort is supposed to breed security, but what it really does is remind you that things could change at any moment, destroying your comfort and forcing change. I've always tried to tell myself that change is a good thing (especially since it's completely unavoidable), but when you've got your cake and can eat it too, who needs change? Change sucks.

After Millie and I got back together, I was a happy man. The physical distance between us was the greatest thing that could have happened to us, in my opinion. We had the best phone chats, revealing so many sides of ourselves. And when we saw each other, the sex was awesome. Oh, it took some getting used to because that little vixen I had spoken about earlier had turned her angry sex into passionate, loving sex that took me away from the world for a while. But like I said, change is inevitable, and I was lucky for a couple of years, until one day I wasn't.

Why can't women just let it be when things are going great? (Because they're not men; that's why.) Millie wanted us to be together, to live in the same city, and I pushed her away. I do love her, but I was afraid of ruining things. The irony of my situation does not escape me since I am the one who committed the act I had so feared. I broke up with Millie because all my words about location not mattering became hogwash. And all my talk about loving Millie's unpredictable side must have also been hogwash, because it was that exact characteristic of hers that prevented me from returning to Miami. What if I had moved my life, my career that I loved, and found myself in deep water with Millie's volatile past? There's my confession...her past has become the wedge between us. I've tried to relate to Millie's suffering, but I can only take it so far. If I even try to imagine a future with Millie and the possibility of having children with her, the heavy weight of the Italian child always suppresses my dreams. Sometimes I wish that child didn't exist, in my guiltiest private thoughts, and I wonder if Millie ever does the same.

In February of 2004, an important event came and went, undetected. My passport expired. Had I been aware or had the need to know, perhaps my story would have been very different, but as I said before, I had become comfortable with the status quo and eventually forgot to question the rules that had been placed on me so long ago. I forgot to ask if anything had changed. I got lazy with acceptance and forgot to investigate new possibilities to solving old problems. Perhaps if Matthew and I had been on a different path at that time—perhaps if we had been planning a wedding and a honeymoon—maybe then things would have been different as I would have had the need to renew my passport. I would have been curious, realizing how many years had passed, and I would have had the courage to call Carlo and perhaps find out that time had healed all wounds. If not, maybe I would have had the strength to challenge the Italian authorities and expose the corruption, or maybe I wouldn't have had to. Maybe Regina had softened with age and would have willingly fixed everything with a wave of her hand…like magic.

It was all conjecture since it took me two more years to have a reason to pull my passport out of the archives of my junk drawer. By that point, a river of water had passed under the bridge between Matthew and me, and he had come back into my life. This story definitely merits further explanation.

In February, while my passport was quietly expiring, Haley and I had the chance to see each other at an ESL educators' convention in Orlando, Florida. We had arranged to share a hotel room together to have plenty of time to catch up, and it was after our first full day of lectures and workshops that Haley had the chance to tell me how quickly Matthew had jumped back into the saddle. "He met Rachel at a New Year's Eve party."

"But that was the day after he got home from Miami!" I was incredulous.

"I know. She's my colleague, but I swear, Millie, I did not set them up."

"So how bad is it?

"She's that super easy-going type who lives life by the seat of her pants and laughs at everything that comes out of a guy's mouth. She knows how to work it." Haley rolled her eyes.

"And I assume she's got a lot to work with," I added.

Haley nodded sadly. "But more than looks, Millie, she just doesn't seem to have a care in the world. She's light and breezy."

Light and breezy. I felt that way once, a long time ago, before Enzo and before Carlo.

Haley retired to the bathroom to clean up for the night, so I plopped onto my hotel bed and let myself remember a day in Bologna, when the light and breezy weather had tried to compensate for my dark and heavy mood.

It was September, and Enzo had just learned to walk. He was about fourteen months old and had those thick, soft legs that young children have before the baby fat gets burned off by the incessant movement of a curious toddler. Carlo, Enzo, and I were in Giardini Margherita to celebrate the second birthday of one of my director's grandchildren. I remember sitting on a blanket on the grass, watching Enzo dart around, fall down hard on his bottom, use both hands to prop himself back up, and dart around some more. He squealed at the joy of being out in the park, and I felt equally stimulated on that surprisingly warm day as I people-watched and enjoyed the antics of the other young celebrants. The birthday girl's aunt became particularly fascinated by Enzo's clownish walk, and she laughed freely every time he fell down. The aunt's name was Annabella, and she was about eighteen years old with long, flowing black hair and those large dark brown eyes that often fill the face of an Italian woman. She was beautiful and seemed to be in love with every child at the party, including her niece, the birthday girl. I think I remember her looks so well because I remember Carlo watching her most of the time. He didn't try to hide his pleasure in watching Annabella move as she bent down to play with Enzo and tossed her long hair over her shoulder, revealing a wide, unabashed smile and full, perfectly-rounded breasts. I was jealous because even fourteen months after giving birth, my figure hadn't yet returned to its original form. I was not terribly overweight but rather softer and a bit wider than I was before I had joined the not-so-exclusive motherhood club. As Enzo rolled around in the grass with Annabella, Carlo commented that she'd make a great babysitter, as if we could have afforded one.

Haley came out of the bathroom and saw me zoned out on the bed. "A penny for your thoughts?"

"I don't think they're worth that much." I sighed. "I guess all the talk about Matthew's light and breezy girl made me think of a time when I felt threatened by a light and breezy girl in Bologna. Carlo was so enthralled with her that he wanted her to become the babysitter. How cliché, no?" Haley laughed, and my mind wandered back to Carlo. "You know, my ex-husband is married now. At least, I assume that he is since he wanted the annulment to be able to re-marry. That was back in 2000."

"Then he's probably married…to the babysitter," Haley commented.

"I wonder if he has another child. Oh my God, Enzo may have a sister or brother!" I shook my head, trying to free it from the images of Carlo's happy little family. For some reason, I saw the expansion of Carlo's family as a stronger barrier against my chances of ever getting Enzo back. But who was I kidding? In reality, I would probably never get my son back, and I told myself that his happiness should be paramount, even if it meant that he was happy having a baby brother or sister. Suddenly, my mind changed its track. "Haley!"

"What?" She jumped when I called her name.

"Instead of just meeting at a three-day conference like this, what do you think about the idea of you and me traveling to Europe together?" I didn't know where the idea had come from, but it sounded like a great one.

"Are you considering trying to visit Italy?"

Actually, I wasn't. As I said, my mind had changed tracks. "No, I was thinking more of Paris or London. But now that you say it, maybe I should look into Italy. It's been so many years since I left. Maybe my notorious status has changed." I raised my eyebrows at the exciting notion.

"Millie." By the tone of Haley's voice, I knew that she was about to burst my bubble. "First of all, I don't have the money to travel to Italy or anywhere else in Europe; I'm not as frugal as you are. And second, you should really check things out with the Italian consulate before you get worked up about something that probably can't happen."

"You are a killjoy, Haley."

The talk of the European vacation became a running joke between Haley and me. About once every other month, I would bring up the idea again, and she would remind me of her limited resources. I would encourage her to start saving, and she would encourage me to go to the consulate. It was the same conversation re-run several times a year, like a syndicated episode of Millie & Haley. Eventually, the talk only needed ellipses as I would begin with, *Why don't we go to Europe?* And Haley would say, *Blah, blah, blah, money. Blah, blah, blah, consulate.* The banter had become so commonplace that we forgot to listen to our own suggestions. Haley never started saving because the idea of the trip was all talk to her, and I never went to the consulate for fear of potentially having to face my demons.

When you think about it, it's really amazing how adaptable we humans are. After almost seven years, my new way of life had become quite bearable. I continued dreaming about a reunion with Enzo, but the act of dreaming had become my life. I wasn't sure that a life with Enzo would actually work, since this life of waiting had come to suit me. I could go through my day without fulfilling any other greater need than my own survival. I could be eternally non-committal, beguiling myself into believing that I was so because I was waiting for Enzo. Since that day would probably never come, the rhythm of my life became one of appearing to be living while actually doing nothing of the sort. I thought of the expression, *Be careful what you wish for. You just might get it.* The words kept ringing in my ears every time I thought about going to the consulate. Being reunited with Enzo was all I had dreamed about since 1997, but that meant that Enzo had grown into a nine-year-old boy over those seven years. He had a life, a family (I presumed), and a world without me. My re-entry would cause nothing but anguish, especially since I was sure that he had been told that he was abandoned by his mamma. I couldn't imagine Carlo or Regina willing to be the fall guy, which would put me in the position of telling Enzo that his babbo and nonna were liars...cruel and ruthless liars. Somehow, I didn't see my accusations going over well or being corroborated by anyone. My only hope for returning to Enzo would be the death of somebody...I wasn't sure who. So I stayed away from the Italian consulate because the demons were more powerful than my little cloud angel.

The 2004 hurricane season proved to millions of Americans that we had messed with Mother Nature for far too long, and the state of Florida was the first to be punished. I had grown up in Miami and could only twice recall having to evacuate my home because of a hurricane threat. The first was in 1980 for Hurricane David, a storm that came close to making landfall but turned away at the last moment, leaving South Florida dry and unscathed. The second was in 1992 for Hurricane Andrew, a storm that passed directly over Miami and its southern neighbor, Homestead, and demonstrated the wrath of a woman scorned to a whole new generation of Floridians. Since that time, we knew what the threat of a hurricane meant, or at least we did for a few years until several relatively peaceful hurricane seasons softened us once again.

By August of 2004, Floridians had forgotten what it meant to be hit by such a powerful storm until Charley swept across the west coast from the Gulf of Mexico, followed shortly thereafter by Frances on the east. Ivan came over South Florida in September and made some crazy twists and turns north before returning south to smash the Florida panhandle. South Florida closed its storm season in September with Jeanne, who poured enough water over us to wash away all our dirty sins…for a while.

By the time the winter holidays came, I felt quite used to the feeling of destruction, which was a good thing since the holiday season had proven to be a destructive time in my life. December of 2004 was no exception because when Haley called to let me know about her arrival dates into Miami, she also dropped a bomb. "Matthew's bringing Rachel to Miami with him."

My heart sank.

"Millie, they eloped last week."

I put down the phone and ran into the bathroom to vomit.

After cleaning myself up and properly hanging up the phone so I wouldn't have to listen to the annoying sound it was making, I went to sit out on my balcony. I needed fresh air.

I had really blown that relationship. If I hadn't been so wrapped up in Enzo, I would have been able to love Matthew better, but if I'd been able to stay in Bologna, I would never have met Matthew. I would probably be miserable with Carlo or finally divorced but unable to conquer the world because I had Enzo. But if I had never had Enzo, I would probably be living in some other country, and I wouldn't have met Matthew. Either way, Enzo had to be in my life for me to have met Matthew, and for better or for worse, I had loved my time with Matthew. The sad truth was that I still loved my best friend's brother, but he was now married to another woman, who was light and breezy.

I decided to be the bigger person in my soap opera story, and I called the Crane home in Miami once the Cranes from Syracuse had arrived. "*Mazel Tov*, Matthew!" I wished him Congratulations and Good Luck in Yiddish, the way Jews always do to commemorate a wonderful event.

"Thanks, Millie. It's really great of you to call." Did I sense a somber tone to his voice, or was it my wishful thinking? "How are you?" Matthew asked.

"Doing well," I lied. "Your sister and I are trying to make plans to go to Italy." I don't know what made me say that.

"Really?"

There was an awkward silence until my other line beeped and gave me the perfect out. "Well, Matthew, I just wanted to congratulate you and Rachel, but that's my other line, so I've got to go."

"Sure. Take care, Millie. And thanks again."

I clicked over to the other line to hear Romy blurt out her own wonderful news. "I'm pregnant!"

This time I was genuinely happy to shout out, *Mazel Tov*, and I proceeded to throw a barrage of curious questions her way. I found out that the baby would be due in August. Yes, they were going to find out the sex if they could. Yes, she intended on breast feeding. Yes, she was telling everyone even though she was only six weeks pregnant. And yes, she was more excited than words could say. So was I because I needed to have some joy in my life even if it would come vicariously through my sister's child.

CHAPTER 4

▼

Yesterday I called my wife by the wrong name. I don't even remember what we were arguing about, but I know we were arguing...it's what we do lately. Only months into our marriage, and fighting seems to be all we can do. Rachel was making a point whose details I don't even remember (and it was just yesterday) when I found myself so exasperated that I called her Millie. She immediately went silent. I tried to defend myself, pointing out that I had called her Millie in a moment of frustration—not passion, but my defense rested on deaf ears.

Truth be told, my argument was weak, since I know as well as the next guy that exasperation with a woman and passion are often one in the same. I can only feel exasperated with someone I care about, and the way Rachel was going on, she reminded me somehow of Millie, who is ever-present in my heart.

When I'm alone and my thoughts are my only companion, I can acknowledge that my marriage to Rachel is a fraud. I am a fraud. When you're trying to get over a woman, a rebound relationship is supposed to do the trick...not your first marriage. A second marriage, maybe. But not a first.

In my life, things tend to happen at the same time, leaving other months of my personal calendar empty and uneventful. December had always been a negative month for me, while July had always been a love-hate time of my year. It provided me with beautiful memories and tragic ones intertwined such that in June, I never knew if I should dread the approach of July or celebrate it.

As July of 2005 approached, I felt my stomach turn each time I caught a glimpse of my hanging wall calendar. June 27th, June 28th, June 29th…impending doom on the horizon. Romy's baby shower was being given by David's sister and mother, who had courteously asked my mother and me to co-host but who had also made it clear that, on the invitation, our names would be more symbolic than anything else. They had very definite ideas of how they wanted to run the show but felt that we should not be excluded, so I had basically done nothing as my role of co-hostess apart from marking the date on my calendar…July third—the Sunday after my private birthday celebration with Enzo.

It was a holiday weekend, so many out-of-town members of David's would be at the shower. Romy's mother-in-law had called to ask me if I could help with some decoration preparations on Saturday, July second. I politely refused. I couldn't comfortably explain my previous obligation, but suffice it to say, my refusal did not put me on good terms with the woman. Though Romy complained about my creating tension with her mother-in-law, I assured her that she had no idea of what mother-in-law tensions felt like. That Saturday was my time…time for me to go to the beach and watch Enzo's birthday party from across the ocean. Since his birthday fell on Friday that year, I was sure that he'd be celebrating on my own birthday instead. Like it or not, the timing of my son's birth just one day before my own would forever unite us in a secret bond.

I had successfully made it through July first, July second, and Romy's baby shower on July third when my phone rang on July fourth, Independence Day.

"Hi, Millie."

It was Matthew. I had been standing when I answered the phone, but now I sat down on the sofa. He made my knees weak. "Hey, you," I responded with a cheery voice.

"Happy Independence Day!"

"Thanks," I said, thinking that this couldn't possibly be the reason for his call. Then I added, "Happy Independence Day to you too."

"Actually, it *is* my independence day, but I don't feel so happy about it."

What in the hell did that mean? It sounded like a lead-in for me to inquire, so I did. "Why is it your independence day?'

"Because I'm independent again. Yesterday, Rachel left."

"Oh, I'm sorry." And I felt it. Despite my selfish pleasure, I was really very sorry that Matthew seemed in pain.

"Do you want to know what sucks the most about it?" He asked.

"All right."

"I wasn't even married a year. It's almost like it never happened."

"But it did happen. Was it at least good while it lasted?" I was trying to find the positive for him, which is when I realized that he wasn't sad about losing Rachel but rather about making the wrong choice.

"It was fun before we were married, but then it was just boring. I lost interest, and she felt neglected. Can you believe all this happened in only six months? It was like a high school relationship. What the hell was I thinking? She was the type of girl you date, not marry."

I didn't know what to say, and I wasn't sure why he was calling me. "Matthew?"

"Yes?"

With my kindest voice I asked, "Why are you telling me all this?"

A moment of silence. "I've had a terrible revelation, Millie. And I say terrible, because there is probably no resolution to my problem."

"I'm listening."

"I think I married Rachel to spite you. Is that the pettiest thing you've ever heard, and the most pathetic?"

"Tell me more."

"I'm angry at you. And I love you. And I want to be with you. But I don't want to change my life for you. I'm selfish. And I love you. But I don't even know if you still feel the same for me. And I don't know what to do about it."

Wow. I let the silence bear the weight of the tension between us because I wasn't sure where to go with it.

"This was very tough for me to say, Millie. Please say something."

"Okay. I'm angry at you too. And I love you too. And I want to be with you too. But I'm selfish too. And a reunion with my son will always be my priority. And I don't know what to do about it either."

"At least we're agreeing to disagree. You really still love me?" Matthew asked with such honest vulnerability that I felt very secure in letting him have my deepest thoughts.

"How I wish we weren't having this conversation over the phone, but yes, Matthew. I still love you. I've known that I loved you since the first time we broke up and you were out of my life. I realized how foolish I'd been and how wrapped up I'd been in my obsession to get back Enzo. So I tried to lighten up, but I can't. It's not who I am at this point in my life. I still dream regularly about my son and our reunion. I also dream about you because I want you in my life so badly, but I don't now how to make it work."

Matthew laughed, but it was the kind of laugh that releases tension and softens the lines of communication. Then he asked the question that had to be asked. "So which one of us is going to budge?"

I chose the cop out answer. "Let's see you get divorced first. Then, at least, we'll be on equal footing and we can make that decision face to face."

Hurricane season, 2005: too much mayhem for one sub-tropical state. Hurricane Dennis came in July to start us off with a fresh reminder of what a good smack in the face feels like. Fortunately, Daniel came on August 6, 2005, but he was not a hurricane. He was my nephew. Daniel looked exactly like Romy, which meant that his family resemblance reminded me of Enzo. Truth be told, any baby boy would have reminded me of Enzo, but seeing my nephew brought the memories closer to home.

Eight days later, Daniel had his *bris*, the Jewish rite of passage that my son had been denied. As I listened to the service and the story behind the tradition, I realized something strange…I didn't care about what I was hearing. I became suddenly irritated by the idea that the same dogma of religion to which I had felt so devoted was the wedge that had driven me away from my son. Enzo Mazzini was my son as much as Daniel was to Romy, and it didn't matter to me that Enzo hadn't passed through any Jewish rites or that he probably never would. It didn't matter to me that Enzo was a Catholic who had most likely already taken his first communion. None of it mattered. If I could ever have Enzo back in my life, I would love him no matter his religion. If that meant that I had to tolerate a hanging crucifix in his bedroom, I would do it, and if, God forbid, Enzo had been brainwashed into hating Jews, I would spend the rest of my life teaching him tolerance and always loving him, if he would let me.

Suddenly, I wanted nothing more than to talk to Matthew, but I knew that I had to wait. Matthew would call when the time was right for us to discuss our future.

Two days later, classes resumed at FIU. Fall semester was always the busiest, and my teaching load was at its maximum. I was also a part of the evaluating committee, helping to place incoming students into the appropriate level of their English program, so my daily life had returned to its constant state of movement. I was so wrapped up in work that I forget to think about life, or Matthew.

On the Thursday before Labor Day weekend, Matthew called my cell phone and reached me on my lunch break. "I'm a divorcee, like you."

"Mazel Tov!" I felt my own wide smile as onlookers assumed I had just received some good news, and they were right.

"Can you come up this weekend?"

My smile disappeared so quickly that I felt tension in my brow. "Are you kidding me? On Labor Day weekend you want me to book a last minute ticket?"

"Yeah, I do."

Matthew sounded irritated, so I relaxed my approach. "We have all the time in the world to make things right, Matthew. Classes have just started, and I need to get so many things in order. What if I promise to come up in two more weekends? Would that prove my devotion to working this out?"

"It would be a good start."

I could almost hear him smiling.

"Great. Then I'll e-mail you my flight info as soon as its booked, which I'll do this weekend." Then I added, "I love you, and I'm very happy for us."

"Me, too. I'll count the days."

My trip to Syracuse was postponed due to Katrina. Who was she, you ask? Perhaps another girl in Matthew's life? Not at all. Katrina was the hurricane whose September arrival brought her in from the Atlantic Ocean, across South Florida as a Category One storm, into the Gulf of Mexico, and up to the Louisiana and Mississippi gulf coasts as a Category Four. Her final landfall flooded the Mississippi Delta and erased the historic city of New Orleans from the map as America had known it. We South Floridians felt somewhat petty as we complained about our property losses, missed school days, and lost work opportunities while residents of New Orleans sat on their rooftops, watching bloated corpses float by and fill the air with the stench of death.

After Hurricane Katrina, I thought I could see a trip to Syracuse on the horizon, but Rita put me in my place. Who was Rita? (Need you ask?) After Hurricane Rita, I was too exhausted to think about traveling, yet escaping South Florida and the stress of backed up work was the most enticing proposition, which encouraged me to hop a plane to New York by early October.

On the Friday night that I arrived in Syracuse, I enjoyed an amazing dinner with my best girlfriend and my two-time ex-boy-friend. It was so much fun because the three of us laughed like we never had, mostly because the tension of the past months had been bearing on us all like a freight train. On a daily basis, Haley and Matthew had heard about the chaotic state of Florida from their parents, and Matthew had been hearing it from both ends when he would call to check up on me. I hated to complain, yet I had nothing else to talk about with the all-consuming stress of feeling that we all were being punished by the angriest Mother in the world.

It was therefore all the more exciting when my one true girlfriend announced her engagement to her own on-and-off again beau, Adam. The wedding was set for March of 2006. Like a true lifer in the field of education, Haley had looked for a vacation period that would not interfere with honeymoon plans but that would still give her plenty of time to plan a wedding, and Spring Break at Syracuse had won the bid. To date, it was one of the best nights of my life as I could celebrate both my best friend's joy and my own reunion with the man I loved.

Matthew and I spent the rest of the weekend sitting around the table and talking like business associates trying to work out a very important merger. All the elements were there to be decided: location, finances, and concessions. Who would relocate? Who would jeopardize their career? Who would give in? It was a struggle, but Matthew decided that he would have the better chance of finding good work by returning to Miami than I would by moving to Syracuse. His parents and my family were in Miami, which was certainly a plus. The only thing that each of us needed to do was have patience as Matthew went through the process of job hunting. If I had learned nothing else during the past eight years of waiting for Enzo, I had learned patience.

I had been home from Syracuse for several days, and I was missing Matthew terribly. The low pressure in the sub-tropical atmosphere was exacerbating my easily irritated sinuses, and I had headaches every day. I would look up at the heavy gray clouds and consider my own relocation to upstate New York. Could harsh winters be any worse than these brutal summers that lasted well into October? Things couldn't remain this miserable for much longer, and just when I was sure that the weather was about to change, I was proven right.

On October 24, 2005, Hurricane Wilma came off the Gulf of Mexico, crossed Florida from west to east, and threw South Floridians for one final, seasonal tailspin. Miami had already been hammered by Katrina, and so it was only fair that the county just north of us should suffer Wilma's wrath. And it was big. The Miami-Fort Lauderdale metropolitan area was like Bologna in August…closed for business. Schools and universities were closed. Entertainment events were cancelled. Airports and seaports were closed. Gas stations were empty. The latter was really the impetus for all the other closures since without electricity, nobody could get gasoline, which meant that nobody could travel to school, work, concerts, or far off places where they could find air conditioning or clean, running water.

From my perspective, bitter cold winters were looking rather sweet, but by Halloween, Matthew had convinced me that the weather was changing everywhere. He said that we should not let a few bitchy women (Katrina, Rita, and Wilma) mess up the fun for everyone else.

CHAPTER 5

▼

Back in the 1970s, there was a song called *Rollercoaster*, which compared love to a rollercoaster ride. When I was a kid, I heard the words but thought only of the carnival ride I knew and loved. It wasn't until recently that the song had any meaning to me—a meaning that Millie has helped realize. I've said it before…Millie's unpredictability keeps me afloat. Occasionally, I begin to sink when she rocks the boat and it begins to take on water, but usually I enjoy the wavy ride on the good ship Millie.

We're together again, which means a lot to me but also worries me. I've decided to be flexible and search for my true home within Millie. My job search has begun, and my parents couldn't be happier; I'm going back to Miami, and I'm going to be with Millie. So why am I so worried? Regarding my reference to the boat…I sense a change in the winds and the tides, and that could either beach me on a sand bar or suck me out to sea.

As I have said before, important events in my life have inevitably coincided, oftentimes with the unfortunate impact worthy of a comet colliding with Earth. Matthew's job hunt was not bearing fruit as quickly as he and I had hoped, and it wasn't until March of

2006, two weeks before Haley's wedding, that a job offer made its way to the table. The day that Matthew received his offer in writing, I received a letter from Bologna with a return address from Mazzini on Via Castiglione.

I walked to my bedroom and sat down on the edge of my bed, debating what to do. It was not as simple as just opening the letter and reading it. This letter had to carry significant news because the envelope was heavy as if it contained many pages. I needed to physically place myself in the best position to receive it appropriately, and after many minutes, I moved over to the center of my bed and seated myself in the cross-legged pose. I gently tore open the envelope and laid the letter out neatly in front of me to reveal several pages that appeared to be written in a woman's handwriting. I was afraid to read it. I debated calling Matthew and telling him what was going on, but I decided that whoever had taken the time to write such a long letter to me deserved my private viewing. You might wonder how I could be so patient and not just tear through the letter like a starved person eating food for the first time in days, but I sensed that a life change was coming and I was scared. I leaned back against my headboard and listened to nothing but the hum of the air conditioner, which soothed me with its low and constant murmur. Before I could realize it, I had fallen into a dream about a little cloud angel who sang *My Favorite Things.*

I awoke almost one hour later to find the letter still sprawled out on my bed. I took a deep breath and picked up the first page. It was written in English, though it addressed me in my Italian name.

Dear Emilia,

I apologize for taking so long to write this letter, but I only learned about your true story a few painful weeks ago. Since then, I have struggled with the decision of what to do with my new information and how to go about it. First, let me introduce myself.

My name is Annabella Salvatore di Mazzini, and I am Carlo's wife. I actually saw you many years ago at my niece's birthday party when Enzo was just a baby, and I remember that I thought you looked like a nice lady, which is why it was always so hard for me to understand why you had abandoned Enzo. I hope you will forgive me because, as I said before, I just learned the truth very recently. You see, soon after you left Italy, Carlo hired me as Enzo's nanny. I was starting the university at that time, so it was a good job for me. Plus, I love kids, and Enzo was so adorable! Very soon after starting to work for Carlo, I fell in love with him. I was young, and he was so handsome. He told me all the things I wanted to hear and none of the things that I didn't. He said that he wanted to marry me but that he was still legally married to his wife, who had abandoned him to return to the United States. When you finally agreed to annul the marriage, we got married.

Things have been nice since then as I love Enzo so much and I get along well with Mamma Regina, who I know was always difficult with you. (You don't have to be a genius to figure out that she thought very little of you. It's not that she spoke of you much, but when she did, her bitterness was apparent.) But Mamma Regina has been chronically ill since I have known her. The doctors have still not been able to diagnose her condition, but Carlo tells me that it all began right after you left. Mamma has been suffering from various pains all over her body, high blood pressure, migraine headaches that she never used to get before, and muscle spasms that sometimes cripple her for days.

Mamma's condition changed drastically a few months ago when she was diagnosed with lung cancer, which brings me to how I learned your truth. A couple of weeks ago, they started giving Mamma morphine to help manage her pain. She drifts in and out of sleep, but she is very talkative when she's lucid. What is strange is how emotional and sentimental she has become during her waking hours. She tells me how beautiful I am, which she never used to do, and she verbalizes her love for Carlo, Enzo, and me, another new occurrence.

One afternoon, while Carlo was at work and I was giving her a sponge bath, she began to talk about you. She was crying through most of it, so it was hard for me to understand, but I knew that she was confessing to something awful. I learned that you had left Bologna to visit your sick father in Miami, and while you were gone, Mamma had arranged for you to never return. Through her brother in Rome, she had arranged for a false police report to document your attempt to kidnap Enzo and take him to America. She told me that she had paid off the appropriate authorities to accept the false report and have sole custody awarded to Carlo. She knew about the misclassification of your charge as a conviction, but she chose to do nothing about it. Of course, I was shocked to learn all this, and I asked her why she was telling me this, and she started to cry. She wouldn't answer me, but hours later she told Carlo and me that she was tired of all the sickness and wanted to die soon.

I think she told me to try to cleanse her soul, which you probably think is impossible. But Mamma Regina has been a good nonna to Enzo, and they say that all people deserve God's forgiveness.

After that day, Mamma never spoke of you again, but I did ask Carlo about it, and I was disgusted to hear him confirm her story and admit to knowing about it from the beginning. Oh, I threatened him with many bad things if he didn't make amends to you, but my threats did nothing more than cause terrible fighting and tension, which Carlo said was very bad for Mamma. So I sat with my information, not knowing what to do with it until I got a sign from God.

Three days ago, I found out that I am pregnant for the first time. It has been a long struggle for me to get pregnant, so I believe that God is trying to tell me that it is my time to be someone else's mamma and your time to be Enzo's mamma. Please believe that I love Enzo very much, but I told Carlo that Enzo deserves to know his real mamma just like our baby will know his own mamma. Carlo fought me, but I took a risk and threatened to leave him and go back to my family if he wouldn't let you back into Enzo's life. He gave in, but two problems remained. First, we needed to contact Uncle Salvatore, have your criminal record expunged, and restore your residency status. And second, Carlo insists that we come up with another story for Enzo because Carlo absolutely refuses to be turned into the bad guy, nor does he want Mamma Regina to suffer any more than she already has. Because Enzo is only ten years old, I support my husband on this request.

As I write this letter, Uncle Salvatore is clearing up the legal issues, so here is my proposition for you, Emilia. If you still want to be part of Enzo's life, we will tell him that after you left to visit your family, you went through some rough times and couldn't return to Italy (which I'm sure is not a complete lie.) I realize that you end up taking the blame, but I believe that as Enzo gets older and becomes more able to handle more information, the truth will unfold. If you are willing to not blame Carlo or Mamma Regina (as long as she lives), you will be welcome back to Bologna, either to visit or to remain.

I hope you will consider my proposition because I really think that you would be valuable in Enzo's life, especially as this new phase of his family begins. How special it would be for him to find out that he is getting both a baby brother or sister AND his own mamma, all in the same year.

With my sincerest regards and apologies for my husband and mother-in-law,
Annabella

Annabella: daughter of my ex-director, Carlo's fantasy babysitter, nanny to my son, present wife of my ex-husband, soon-to-be mother of his second child, and Regina's caretaker and confidante. Was she also my salvation?

I read her proposition again. My thoughts were running wild in my mind, colliding with each other and exploding. I picked up the phone and called Romy. "I've just received a letter from Bologna…I can see Enzo."

I had to pull the receiver away from my ear for the squeals that were coming through the other end. "My God, Millie! This is the day you've been anticipating forever! Why don't you sound more excited?"

"Of course I'm excited, but there are provisions, and you're never going to believe who Carlo married?"

Romy demanded that I hang up and drive over to her place immediately so that she could see the letter for herself and we could talk about the next plan of action.

"What about Matthew?" Romy asked me as she walked into the nursery to put Daniel down for a nap.

I was comfortably seated on her living room sofa, my legs curled up beneath me. I was sipping my favorite comfort drink—hot chocolate—and I awaited Romy's return to the living room before trying to verbalize my thoughts. When she had re-situated herself next to me on the sofa, I tried to express the chaos that still raced around inside my head. "They say that timing is everything in life, and I've always believed that."

Romy nodded in agreement.

"Matthew and I certainly have not had the best timing in life. Something tells me that I have to trust my gut, and my gut says to go to my son. If Matthew and I are meant to be together, then the fates will find a way of bringing us to that point. I have no idea how, but I have to believe that it will happen."

"Oh, Millie. I don't envy your position, but I'm so happy for you that you'll get to see Enzo again. If I feel that confused, I can only glimpse the surface of how confused you must feel."

My eyes started to tear as I realized my terrible predicament. "I really love Matthew, and I so wanted to finally be with him." I stopped talking to grab a tissue from the box that Romy always kept on the coffee table to clean up baby spills. "But I've waited for nine damn years to see my son again!"

My shouting surprised me, and I giggled. Romy laughed too and leaned in to hug me. "I can't imagine ever being separated from Daniel. Your strength these past years has been more than admirable. So I think you're right. If you and Matthew are meant to be together, it will happen...somehow."

After bringing my parents up to speed, my next important phone call was to Matthew. "If I could see Enzo but it would mean putting our relationship on hold, how would you feel about it?" I didn't really know how to break the news and had chosen the indirect route.

"This doesn't sound so hypothetical to me, Millie. What makes you think you can see Enzo?"

"I got a letter today. Carlo's wife wrote to tell me that everything's been cleared up and I'm free to return to Italy to see my son." It hurt me just to tell Matthew, but it also warmed me inside to repeat the words that I had already told Romy and my parents.

"Just like that, huh? Everything's been cleared up. Why the change of Italian heart?" He sounded doubtful and, I assumed, hurt.

"Apparently, Carlo's wife just found out the true story of my departure, and she has made Carlo reverse everything, to sum it all up." I had to admit, it sounded too easy...erasing the problems of the past nine years with not much more than a phone call. "I'd love to show you the letter, Matthew, so you can see what's been going on."

"So what does this mean for us, Millie?" He sounded empty.

"It means that I have a lot of thinking and reorganizing to do. There are two things that I am quite sure of, Matthew. The first is that I'm going to see my son again. The second is that I love you."

"But the two cannot coexist, Millie. Your son is in Italy, and I am here."

I had to keep my cool. "Matthew," I took a deep breath. "I have to believe that we are going to be together, somehow. Since we met in 1998, we've been on and off, up and down, and in and out of each other's lives. For some reason, we haven't been able to get it together for eight years, until now, and then life goes and throws another wrench into our plans. But we're both very strong-willed people, and if we're willing to let life beat us at this relationship game, then we should forfeit now."

"What do you want from me, Millie?" Matthew yelled.

I kept my voice calm. "I want to take a sabbatical and go to Italy for one year. I want to see what kind of relationship I can develop with my son before I return to Miami and become the long-distance, once-a-year mommy. If the rest of my motherhood is going to be based on summer visits only, I first need some strong footing to bond with my son. In my perfect world, you would come visit me during my stay in Bologna, and then when I come home next year, we would be together. Do you think our relationship has enough glue to hold itself together through another long-distance year?"

"I don't know."

Given the bomb that I had just dropped on Matthew, I had to cut him some slack. Although we didn't speak for the next week, I wasn't angry with him. I knew that he needed his own space and time to work it all out in his head. I also knew that his job offer wasn't going to wait around forever and that a man tends to need more professional security than a woman. Whatever Matthew was working out during our week of silence, I would never punish him for it.

On my end of things, that week was the most productive of my life. I renewed my passport. I put in my request for a sabbatical, for which I was fully entitled. I booked a Bologna apartment rental on line and had confirmed the details with a local agent. I went to the Italian consulate (finally!) to confirm my open status and, sure enough, received permission for re-entry into Italy. I arranged to sublet my Coral Gables apartment for one year, making a mental note to finally purchase my own place once I returned to Miami. Last, but not least, I booked my flight to Milan for May eighth, which was the first flight available after my spring semester final exam period would be over.

I had two months to wait before being reunited with Enzo, and though Romy and my parents thought I was insane to wait (lest Carlo change his mind), I knew that I could handle two months with no trouble if I had survived nine years. I wanted my life to be as in order as possible before throwing emotional turmoil into the formula. I needed to be free of any American worries in order to have my head together in Italy. I needed to resolve things with Matthew before leaving, and I was hoping, more than I wanted to admit, that some miracle would keep Matthew in my life. I also needed time to prepare Enzo's gift. I wanted to find the perfect accompaniment for my journal, which I intended to give him as proof of my never-ending love and devotion to the little boy that I had left behind.

Two weeks after receiving my letter from Annabella, Haley and Adam got married in Miami. The wedding was a strange time because while Matthew should have been full of joy for his sister, he was preoccupied with me. I should have been full of joy for my best friend, but I was preoccupied with Matthew. Because of the nuptials, Matthew and I had no time together, which was oddly appropriate, given the circumstances. We really had very little to discuss. The wedding weekend zoomed by so quickly that I was back into my waiting period routine before I knew what had hit me.

The time between March and May was tougher than I had imagined, mostly because Matthew had decided not to accept the Miami job offer. He said that it seemed a risky move to make when his local job was stable but the Miami forecast was not. I didn't begrudge him the decision, as personally promised, but I realized that our commitment had suffered a blow, which hurt my heart. Strangely enough, our phone talks were open and loving, helping to restore my trust in the man whose love gave me the confidence to face my son. Matthew had arranged to come to Miami during the last weekend in April for a final visit before I left. I counted the days until his arrival with more anticipation than I did the days until my European departure. After all, it was easier to feel optimistic about Matthew's love than it was to envision Enzo's.

When Matthew finally arrived, he seemed to have renewed energy. Instead of feeling somber about my leaving, Matthew behaved like a man with a special secret that he was dying to share yet determined to keep. His moments of giddiness worried me, and I actually asked him if he was taking amphetamines. He, of course, denied it and said nothing more than that he, too, had faith that we were going to be all right. It was an odd time spent with Matthew, and as I kissed him good-bye in Miami International Airport, he leaned close to my ear and whispered, "See you soon, my love."

I drove home from the airport in silence. I usually listened to the radio when alone in my car, but today I wanted to reflect. Matthew had just left me with the most comforting words I could have wished to hear. His message meant that he would wait for me and be there for me. It meant that he was supporting me and providing the security I needed to enjoy my year in Italy with Enzo. I knew that the next time I was at that airport, it would be to fly to Bologna, and I suddenly felt so high that I had to pull off the road and take deep breaths. As the afternoon traffic whizzed by me, I realized exactly where I needed to be at that moment.

Twenty minutes later, I was surrounded by sand and the smell of the tide. I looked across the ocean and whispered to Enzo, "See you soon, my love."

Millie Gossett will be the death of me yet. It's been a long road that I've traveled with her, but I have no choice. She's the real deal for me, though it's taken me several years and a brief marriage stint to figure that much out. Millie wants me to wait just one more little year, one more teensy little year until we can be together so she can go and become the mother of her own dreams. I was certainly angry at first because enough is enough, you know? But the explorer in me has resurfaced, and I've decided that this year could turn out to be the best thing that ever happened to me. I'm not going to take that job in Miami. Why should I? Millie won't even be there. No, I've got bigger fish to fry while Millie jet sets across the ocean to live the good life. She thinks that she's got the upper hand on dropping bombs on me. Well, she's about to feel an explosion that will rock her world.

PART III
ENZO

CHAPTER 1

▼

The blue, imitation-fleece airline blanket is almost as soft as Enzo's baby blanket, but not soft enough to lull me into sleep, so I continue to chew my fingernails until I have bitten them all down to the quick. This is where you found me at the beginning of my story. I know I look pathetic, but all that serenity I felt when Matthew left Miami flew away quicker than the pilot could say, "Flight attendants, prepare for takeoff."

For several hours, I have been dying to talk to someone to help relieve my stress and keep my fingers away from my mouth, but the lady seated next to me has made it very obvious that she is not the chatty type. She has been engrossed in her novel or her movie or her restful sleep for the entire trip, while I have been jealous. Sure, I brought a book to read. I tried watching the in-flight movie, but my fingers suffered their most damage during those one hundred minutes. There's a gentleman seated on the aisle seat opposite mine, and he looks rather friendly. Unfortunately, his wife is at his side, and she gives me the evil eye any time I try to make eye contact with the man to initiate small talk. So, I've been alone this whole journey, except for you. You've been a great audience, listening to my story without judging or, at least, without letting me hear your judgment, and I appreciate that. Since you've come this far with me, you might as well continue and come meet my son, Enzo. We'll be arriving in just one hour, so sit back and pray for a smooth landing.

I land in Milan without incident, hoping for the same luck as I pass through Customs. Despite having confirmed my passport clearance with the Italian authorities in Miami, I am still apprehensive. I approach passport control, and the agent takes my passport, scanning it and then thumbing through the pages until he comes to my temporary permit. He reminds me that I must report to the local authorities upon arrival in my final destination to receive my permanent permit. I nod in affirmation, knowing exactly to what he is referring. He returns my passport with a quick smile and a *Prego,* the all-purpose word for please, pardon, and you're welcome. I am officially in Italy, and I practically skip my way to the train station as I push my heavy cart full of luggage.

I pass the two-hour train ride from Milan to Bologna in a deep sleep and only awaken when my cell phone alarm sounds five minutes before my projected arrival time. I catch a taxi along the Viale, the wide road encircling the historic center of Bologna, and I watch life happening outside the window as the cab makes its way up Via dell'Osservanza, one of the many winding streets leading into the hills just outside the Viale. I have rented a guesthouse situated at the entrance to a larger estate, about one kilometer up the road. As the taxi driver makes the slow, uphill ascent, I notice the fourteen Stations of the Cross posted along the way, signaling the stopping points for the miniature pilgrimage that Catholics make during Lent, Holy Week, or Good Friday. My new home is at the fourteenth station, representing Christ being laid to rest. This also means that I am at the peak of my particular hill, offering me a view of the city to one side and the lower hills to the other. Located next to my cottage is Villa Aldini, a neoclassical wonder built under Napoleon's minister in the early 1800s and now a retirement home for those fortunate enough to live atop this crested hill. This is significant because it means that just outside my front door, I can also find a bus stop, which is a scarce treasure beyond the Viale.

Once I have my luggage out of the cab and have paid the driver in euros (a new currency for me to calculate), I leave everything unattended in this pastoral part of town and walk another one-quarter kilometer up a tree-lined driveway to the main house to retrieve my key. My landlady is a lovely woman in her early fifties, and she welcomes me to Bologna, obviously assuming that it's my first time in her beautiful city. I walk back down the driveway, feeling a bit chilled by the breeze that blows stronger in the hills, and I notice the charming patio behind the guesthouse. I immediately decide that there is where I will have my breakfast each morning.

The cottage is two stories tall and is about the size of a small American townhouse. The exterior walls are the perfect shade of terra cotta, and the shutters are painted the same dark green as the wild grass that grows in the surrounding hills. The front door has a varnished wood finish, and as I put in the key and turn it, I feel the heavy weight of the dense wood as it slides open. The entry hallway is tiled in a dark brown ceramic that I later notice runs throughout the cottage. The small kitchen walls are covered in a green and white patterned ceramic, which is carried through in the downstairs half bathroom and the upstairs full bathroom. The only other downstairs room is the salon, which is furnished with a sofa, a desk, a small side table, and a television. I have to walk up a spiral staircase to reach the second floor, where there are three bedrooms, though one of them is so small that nothing but a twin-sized bed and a small armoire fill up the narrow space. The other two rooms each have a queen-sized bed, nightstand and armoire, and from all the bedroom windows I can see a perfect view of the hills below. I decide to take the room that faces the front of the house, which will leave the room that faces the rear for guests, should any choose to visit. The small room will be for Enzo because it's so cozy that I hope it will encourage him to eventually stay with me overnight.

I am very pleased with my little house. I walk back down the tight staircase, go into the salon, curl up on the brick-red, upholstered sofa, and turn on the TV. The white noise of the Italian soap opera lulls me into another deep sleep, and I don't wake up until the following morning.

After unpacking and snacking on the bag of cookies that I purchased in Milan's train station, I take a quick shower and head into town to do some grocery shopping. There is really so much to do before I can even consider contacting Carlo. It's May tenth, and the spring air is still chilly though the sun is glorious. I feel very good to be back, better than I thought I would, and I wonder what will happen if I fall in love with this city again. I spend the better part of the morning shopping and then standing in line at the Office of Immigration to get my permit stamped. The clerk comments on the odd gap in time between my departure in 1997 and my return in 2006, but I just smile politely and say that I needed a really long vacation. He doesn't find the humor in my response and sends me on my way with a gruff *Prego.*

By one o'clock in the afternoon, I know I can phone Matthew. It's seven o'clock in the morning in New York, and he will be getting ready for work on this hump day. He answers the phone with a trace of morning voice, though I know that he's been awake for over an hour already. "*Buongiorno!*" I shout.

"Well, good morning to you too! How was your trip?"

"You didn't care very much for my fingernails, did you?" I ask playfully. "Because I've chewed all ten of them down to their nubs."

"Gross!" Matthew pokes fun at me, but I can hear the smile in his voice. "Have you seen Enzo yet?"

I get serious. "Oh no. I've been so busy this morning doing all those getting-settled things that I haven't even called Carlo. Or maybe I should call Annabella," I say more to myself than to Matthew.

"Good idea. She seems to be your ally."

"Right. Well, I just wanted to let you know that I'm safe and sound. My little house is so precious...you have to come visit soon. Are you still planning on Christmas Break?"

Matthew avoids answering my question and instead asks me if I've ever heard of Rizzoli. I think it's an odd response that has nothing to do with us, but I answer him anyway. "I think it's a small town around here. We can try to find it when you come. You really have to come this Christmas, okay?" I demand an answer this time.

"I promise I'll be there for Christmas."

As I later walk through Piazza Maggiore, I think about Matthew's question. I suddenly remember the name Rizzoli as being connected with a hospital up in the hills, and I imagine that Matthew read about Rizzoli in one of his journals. I make a mental note to take him there for a tour when he comes to visit.

It's not until the late afternoon that I gather the courage to call Annabella to let her know that I'm in town. She's very animated when I identify myself on the phone.

"Emilia! Welcome back!" She actually sounds as nervous as I am.

"*Grazie*," I thank her. "And I don't mean just for the warm welcome."

"I'm just glad that I could make this happen and start to make things right."

"I don't even know you, but I know that you're a good woman, Annabella."

"I'm just trying to do what's best for Enzo." I can almost hear her blushing.

"Does he know I'm coming?" I inquire.

"Yes. As agreed, we told him that you'd be coming this week, and we've tried our best to help him see how we support this reunion."

"Do you think that he wants to see me?"

"Oh, he definitely wants to see you, but I think it's more out of curiosity than anything else."

"Curiosity is good in a child," I am trying to find the silver lining.

"Saturday at Giardini Margherita then? Eleven o'clock, let's say?"

"Who will bring him?" I'm anxious enough without having to add Carlo to this reunion, so I'm hoping that Annabella will be Enzo's escort.

"I will, Emilia. Is that all right?"

"Perfect. And please call me Millie." I feel more relaxed now.

I am walking on the Viale, somewhere between Via San Mamolo and Via Castiglione, and the traffic roars past me along the six-lane wide boulevard. Cars honk loudly, sometimes at each other in anger and sometimes at me in flirtatious greeting. During the daytime, walking the Viale is commonplace, especially near the park, which is where I am headed. But at night, a woman with any self-respect wouldn't be seen on foot on this road; else she would be suspected of prostitution and would certainly make a good living at it if that were her aim.

I can see the black, iron gate that marks the entrance to Giardini Margherita. Though I've never approached the park from this direction, that gate is very familiar. How many times before, years ago, had I passed through that gate without even noticing it? How many times had I crossed its threshold without giving any weight to its symbolism? Over the past nine years, that gate has been locked to me, standing tall and strong with its iron bars that locked my son inside and kept me out. I could only grab onto the gate's bars and hope to glimpse my past, but the trees were always in the way. This morning, that same gate is open to welcome me back to Bologna and to my child. There are trees everywhere, but I can peer through the branches of leaves that blow lightly in the spring breeze, and I can see the world inside. My heart beats strongly, and I have to stop and put my right hand over my chest to calm it down. I realize that I'm in the correct posture to pledge allegiance to the American flag, but at this moment, I feel allegiance to no one but Enzo.

My dear Enzo. What will you look like at almost eleven years old? Will you smile when you see me or run and hide behind your step-mother? Will you shake my hand politely or kiss me on each cheek? Maybe you'll even hug me, and then I'll cry so hard that you'll think me insane. I must keep control of my emotions. I'm smart enough to know that a ten-year-old child cannot begin to fathom adult pain, and he certainly has no idea that I've been living my life solely for him since I said good-bye to a little cloud angel.

I pass through the park gate and let the noises of nature and laughing children shut out the world behind me. In the satchel that I am carrying is Enzo's gift, but I'll only give it to him today if he's receptive to it. I try to put myself in his shoes so that I can be as empathetic as possible to what he must be feeling, but the truth is that I have absolutely no idea in the world of what he feels because I don't know this boy anymore. We're starting a new relationship, not continuing an old one. I must remember this.

As I am about to turn up the paved walkway that leads to the gelato stand, my cell phone rings. I'm shocked by its sound, and I jump at the same moment that I shout, "Shit!" If I had been worried about not being able to receive American calls while in Italy, my cell phone has proven to be well-worth the investment by providing excellent reception, even when I don't want it. The caller ID tells me that it's Haley, and I think that maybe something bad has happened. I stop walking to answer the phone. "Hi, Haley. Is every-thing okay?"

"Have you seen Enzo yet?" Haley is shouting with her own excitement.

"Haley, I'm on my way, right now, so please let me go."

"Okay, go! Kisses…"

I close the phone before Haley can make her kissy sounds.

The call has thrown me off course. My head is somewhere else for a moment, and I want to be focused on this moment, right here and right now, so that I can remember these feelings, whether good or bad, for the rest of my life. I look around before continuing to walk because I'm trying to regain my bearings. Then I see them.

About ten yards ahead, sitting side by side on the park bench closest to the gelato stand, are Annabella and Enzo. How do I know this? Because the woman has that long, flowing black hair that I remember, but her perfectly rounded breasts are now even fuller from her pregnancy, which her belly doesn't quite reveal yet. As for the boy, he has my eyes. Annabella and Enzo are looking in the other direction, and he's even leaning over her lap as if expecting me to come from the other side. I'm still frozen in my spot, and bike riders and skaters occasionally whiz by me. The breeze from their wake chills me, and I decide to walk towards my son. Enzo is wear-ing jeans, a red golf shirt, and black loafers. I think he looks a little too maturely dressed for his age, but then I imagine Annabella dressing him this morning to look his best, which makes me smile. Annabella is wearing a knit dress and flat sandals, and even though she's seated, I can tell that she is elegant.

I continue noticing the fine details of Enzo's features until he suddenly turns and looks right at me. Our eyes lock, and the only thing Enzo can do is reach blindly for Annabella's hand, which causes her to also turn my way. I smile tensely but sincerely and hold that expression until I'm standing no more than eight feet in front of them. I open my mouth to speak, but Annabella stands up suddenly and beats me to the punch. "You must be Millie." I nod once, and Annabella touches my left arm as she leans in for the customary kiss on each cheek. "It's so nice to finally meet you!" Annabella sounds very sincere, and as she turns to Enzo to watch his expression, I turn to him, too.

"Hi Enzo," I say. "I'm—" I don't know if I should say Mamma or Millie.

"I know," he saves me. "You're Mamma. I kind of remember you." The nervousness of his voice and the sound of *Mamma* coming from his lips instantly make my eyes tear. Time seems to be standing still for a moment until Enzo, the little hero, speaks up. "You can hug me if you want."

Then, I forget my promise to control my emotions, and like the dramatic scene in some long-lost lovers' story, I drop to my knees, throw my arms around Enzo's waist, and sob into his chest. My little man hugs my head and even kisses the top of it once. I have been blessed.

After recovering from the greeting, Enzo and I walk to the gelato stand. Annabella has decided to let us be together for a little bit while she roams the park and enjoys some quiet time for herself. When I asked her where Carlo was, she gave me the let's-not-talk-about-that-now look, so I let it go.

As Enzo and I wait in line, I remember the one secret that I know about him. "I'll bet I can guess your favorite flavor of gelato," I say, hoping that his taste hasn't changed with age.

"What is it?" He asks shyly.

"*Nocciola!*" I declare proudly.

Enzo has seen the first proof that mothers know everything, and he is obviously in awe of me. "How did you know that?"

I momentarily debate the idea of leading him to believe that I deserve complete admiration for knowing such important details, but I decide on the truth, which I believe will also prove my devotion to him. "Well, Enzo...Back when you were only about four years old, my sister—your Aunt Romy—was here in Bologna. She wanted to see you so that she could tell me you were all right, so she found you here in the park. She stood in line behind you right in this very spot, and she heard you order *nocciola*, and she told me about it when she returned to Florida."

"Really?" Enzo is curious.

"Really. And you know what else?" I see that my story has captivated him, so I go on. "That day that Aunt Romy saw you, she also spoke to you." I stop and glance around to find the nearest water fountain. When I find it, I continue. "Right over there at that water fountain." I am pointing to the only fountain that I can see, and Enzo's eyes are following my finger.

"What did she say to me?" Enzo asks.

But I am stumped. I don't recall a particular conversation, only that Romy had said that Enzo was well. "She said that you were growing into such a big boy."

Enzo smiles, though it seems forced to me. Just then, it's our turn to order. "I would like a *stracciatella,* please." Enzo looks at me out of the corner of his eye, and it is the first sign of anger that I sense. He has ordered a different flavor of gelato—*stracciatella*—which is like a vanilla cream with little pieces of chocolate in it.

I order the *nocciola* and look Enzo boldly in the eye. "Well, that was always my favorite flavor anyway." Then I flash him one of my most sincere smiles, hoping to win back his favor. I pay for the gelatos and motion with my head for Enzo to follow, and he does. We walk in silence, both eating our gelatos as I come up with a plan. This has been a lot for him, I imagine, and I think that his hint of hostility at the gelato stand should have been expected. I should have realized that he may be carrying a lot of resentment towards me since he believes that I abandoned him. Come to think of it, it would be rather strange if he accepted me at face value. No child should be so trusting, and I'm glad that mine isn't either. Patience is the virtue that I must practice right now, and since I've been practicing for nine years, I'm sure that I'm up to the task now. After all, I've got a year to get to know my son and for him to get to know me, and I'm hoping that he'll eventually find it in his heart to love me in whatever way he can. I finally break our silence with my proposition. "Enzo, I think this gelato was just what I needed."

Enzo nods his head.

"How about we find Annabella and call it a morning for you and me? And if you'd like, I'd love to see you tomorrow after lunch. Could we do that?"

Tomorrow is Mother's Day in the United States, and I've been dreaming of spending mine with Enzo since last March when I received Annabella's letter. I cross my fingers in hopes that Enzo will agree.

"I've got to ask Babbo first."

"Of course." I had completely forgotten about Carlo for a little while; it had been so beautiful to just be with Enzo. But I'm pleased that Enzo seems receptive to my idea. "If your babbo says that it's okay," I start, but Enzo cuts me off.

"Were you and Babbo married a long time ago?" Boom! My son is pulling no punches. He's gone right to the heart of what's on his mind.

"If your babbo says that it's okay," I start again. "Then I promise to tell you anything you want to know...tomorrow."

I think I've enticed him because he's smiling with satisfaction. "*Va bene.*"

As Enzo and I are closing our deal, Annabella finds us. I thank her for her kindness, kiss Enzo on each cheek, and whisper in his ear. "Don't have any dessert tomorrow, *Va be'?*"

Enzo nods once and waves as he and Annabella walk down the paved path, leaving me with my thoughts.

Not until Enzo and Annabella are out of sight do I feel the circulation return to my legs. I walk to the nearest bench and let myself fall onto it like a rag doll. I am emotionally exhausted. I take several slow, deep breaths before pulling out my cell phone and dialing Haley's number. I get her voice mail, curse her for being unavailable, but leave a message anyway, shouting every phrase as if my voice needs to travel from Italy to New York. "I saw my son! I saw Enzo! He's beautiful! We ate ice cream together, and we're probably going to see each other tomorrow, too! I am so happy! Bye! I mean, *Ciao!*"

I sit there on that park bench for a long time because I'm not sure what to do with myself and because I can't move. I don't want to move. I'm afraid that if I leave this bench and walk away from this moment, it might disappear, getting sucked up into some wrinkle of time that will randomly select my moment of joy to erase forever.

I saw Enzo, and he touched me. He kissed my head like I imagine only God would do at the moment of greeting us at the gates of Heaven. Enzo wants to see me again. And although I sense trepidation, it is all beautiful. I have flown across the Atlantic Ocean, soared over Morocco and the Mediterranean Sea, and reached Enzo. It is my dream come true.

It's almost lunchtime but I have no appetite. I decide to roam the grounds of the beautiful gardens and enjoy the first peaceful sensation that I've experienced in years.

CHAPTER 2

▼

How many years have passed since I last heard Carlo's voice? It doesn't really matter anymore. Its timbre and cadence are no more meaningful to me than that of a stranger's. Instead, it is Matthew's voice that rings true in my ears, fills my heart with hope, and comforts me like my own father's once did a time long ago, when *he* was the man with all the answers and before he stopped being there for me. It's amazing how emotionally connected I am to sound. In fact, for nine years I could perfectly hear the pitch and rhythm of Enzo's baby talk, like a crisp memory that sang to me in my dreams. But now that's gone. Now, I've heard the doubtful tones of a pre-adolescent boy whose vocal pitch will all too soon drop out of boyhood and begin the arduous ascent into manhood. That's the sound of Enzo. That's the sound of my son. And if I want to listen to Enzo's voice and learn to interpret its ever-changing nuances, I must speak to Carlo. I must find out if sound can pain me as easily as it soothes.

Later that evening, I make the bold phone call to Carlo, who answers the phone with one simple word. *"Pronto?"* Hello?

Carlo's word lingers in the air and then falls on my ears, but not before it surprisingly touches my heart and makes me yearn for something I hadn't realized that I had missed. I have the strangest desire to freeze time, run back twelve years, and make everything right.

"Good evening, Carlo."

"He recognizes my voice immediately since he's probably been expecting my call all day. "How are you, Millie?"

"I'm great, thanks."

"So, how much do you hate me?" His tone is slightly self-deprecating and slightly sarcastic, and it seems an odd question for our first encounter since my return. I ponder the idea for a second before deciding that Carlo is not going to ruin my wonderful day. Right now, I have no room for hate.

"Carlo, hating you is the farthest thing from my mind. What has been done has been done, and I believe that at least your mamma has paid the price. Right now, Enzo is the only thing on my mind, and I love how I felt today being with him."

"Yes, I heard you had a nice visit."

"Really?" I can't hide my joy at hearing such a review, and then I check myself. "Carlo, can I see Enzo again tomorrow? It's Mother's Day, and I'd like to take him somewhere special."

"What time?"

"Three o'clock? I'll pick him up at your place and we'll take a taxi."

Carlo hesitates before answering. "Please come a little early…Mamma wants to see you." That is not part of my plan. I don't know what to say, and then Carlo speaks again. "She's dying, you know."

I get to Regina's (and Carlo's) place on time, but I'm so tempted to remain outside their building door, under the stately portico. I'm afraid to see Carlo, and I don't want to see Regina. But then I visualize her face as I knew it years ago, and I have a calming revelation…I do not hate Regina Buonsignore. As strange as it sounds, it's true. She has wronged me in the worst way, yet I don't hate her. Instead, I pity her. When I came to understand the pattern of her illness, I interpreted it as her subconscious, self-inflicted punishment. Since I left, her life has been miserable, and she hasn't even had the chance to enjoy her grandson. That honor was given to Annabella, who will now have her own flesh and blood to love. It's not that I doubt Annabella's love for Enzo, but no other mother can love him more than I can. I am Enzo's mamma.

I'm about to ring the buzzer when I suddenly think of Matthew. Though our relationship has been through some crazy times, Matthew has been the one constant in my life almost since my return to Miami in 1997. There's been Haley and, of course, my family, but Matthew has been the man in my life, even when he wasn't there...kind of like Enzo. In a strange way, I owe Regina for my chance to love Matthew.

With a much stronger sense of security, I call up to my son's house. I walk up the stairs and find the front door slightly ajar, awaiting me. Enzo greets me with a smile and a *Ciao*, and Annabella shouts out a *Ciao* from the kitchen. I'm still in the small foyer as painful memories of dreaded visits become so vivid. The apartment smells the same (and why shouldn't it?), and the furniture is the same. But the energy is not the same. With death lingering outside the door, a different kind of negative energy fills the air.

"Millie!" Carlo shouts as he enters the foyer from the kitchen and leans in for the double kiss. "It's great to see you again." He sounds a bit too enthusiastic, given our history, so I smile wryly but say nothing. His demeanor seems grossly inappropriate, and I don't know what to do about it. Carlo steers me into the kitchen, where Annabella has just left to tend to Regina. As I remember the one beautiful moment that Regina and I shared over coffee and an ultrasound photograph, Carlo sits down at the small dining table and motions for me to do the same. "I just want to clarify," he begins.

·

"Enzo thinks that you left when he was two years old because your father was ill, and you couldn't come back because you had to help your mother take care of your father. You never came back because you were going through some difficult times…you know, emotionally."

"You mean to say that I was unstable? Crazy?"

Carlo shrugs his shoulders as if to say, *However you want to interpret it,* and the first shoe drops.

"What the hell does that mean to a child of Enzo's age? I mean, if he asks me what was so difficult that I couldn't come back to him, what am I supposed to say?"

Carlo looks at me with a flat expression. "You're creative, Millie. You'll come up with something."

I sit back in the chair and sigh loudly. "There's a question that I've been asking myself for many years, Carlo. When did you start hating me so much? Was it before or after Enzo was born?"

Carlo seems to contemplate my question before responding. "I never hated you, Millie. In fact, I loved you. But I did lose faith in you probably around the time of Enzo's baptism."

I cannot avoid letting a single laugh escape me. "Do you know when I had the most faith in you, Carlo? The day I told you I was pregnant, and you stood outside Zanetti and told me that you wanted our baby to learn whatever I wanted him to learn, even if it was Judaism."

"I don't remember saying that." Carlo speaks so honestly, but it makes no difference.

"The thing is, Carlo. I've come to realize that it doesn't matter what God Enzo prays to, and I just wish I had seen how unimportant it really was back then. I love him. That's all."

"But it is important."

I put up an open hand to say stop. "One last question, please. Have you taught Enzo to hate Jews?"

Carlo looks appalled. "I do not hate Jews, Millie. It was Mamma who always spoke that way."

"And did she speak that way around Enzo?"

Carlo shakes his head. "With you out of the picture, she had no reason to discuss Jews at all."

"Good." I stand up. "I'm going to say hello to Regina now, but I have one last thought for you. Have you ever considered contacting your father's relatives in Rimini? I mean, it's been a long time...a lot of water under the bridge. Maybe Enzo could meet some Mazzini cousins."

"It's pointless," Carlo says. "I wouldn't even know where to begin to find them."

I turn to walk out of the kitchen but cannot resist giving him a piece of advice. "You could start by checking with the closest synagogue to Rimini."

Although I have turned my back on Carlo without giving him the chance to respond, I can hear the other shoe dropping.

Regina is in her bedroom, propped up in bed with many pillows supporting her back and head. When I enter the room, I am unexpectedly shocked by her appearance. I've been fortunate to have never seen a cancer sufferer, so I have no idea how deteriorated they can look. Though she's only sixty-two years old, she appears to be one hundred. Her already thin face has gotten thinner, and I can see the structure of her cheek bones and her jaw. She apparently lost her hair a while back, and it's slowly growing back as thin silver slivers of hay. My eyes tear up as I see her. Nobody should have to suffer as badly as that...not even Regina Buonsignore.

When Annabella sees me, she quietly steps out of the bedroom, leaving me alone with my ex-mother-in-law.

"Hi, Regina." I greet her informally, trying to sound friendlier than I feel.

Regina opens her eyes, which periodically close even though she is awake. She sees me and recognizes me instantly. "The Jew," she says, but this time she's trying to smile. She then adds a compliment. "The beautiful Jewish girl."

Something has softened about Regina's tone and manner, and I sadly assume that it has to do with facing death and trying to repent for wrongdoings.

"How are you?" Though it's obvious, I feel that it's appropriate to pretend that it isn't and walk us through the niceties.

"I've been better," she tries to laugh. "I'm glad you came to see me."

I nod once.

"You must hate me, Emilia. I certainly deserve it."

I shake my head. "No, I don't."

Regina suddenly seems angry. "How can you not hate me? Are you so weak that you can't even show me your anger?" She coughs violently from raising her voice, and I wait patiently for the coughing to subside.

"Actually, Regina. I'm not weak at all. In fact, I am strong, and I owe my strength to you."

She looks confused.

"If you had not robbed me of my motherhood, I would never have figured out who I am and found true love."

"You are still a silly dreamer," she says, trying to sound bitter but too weak of voice to pull it off.

"No, I'm a pragmatist. You put me in a terrible situation, and I've simply found the silver lining. If I hadn't been able to do that, I would have lost my mind." Regina says nothing, and I take the opportunity to ask her the question that she originally asked me. "Do *you* still hate *me*?"

Regina looks me in the eye before answering. "I'm too tired to hate. There's no more room for it in here." She touches her chest.

"Well, I forgive you, Regina. I just want you to know that."

With her tired hand still resting on her chest, Regina can't seem to move. Her eyes fill up with tears, and she closes them tightly.

"Are you all right?" I start to panic.

Regina lifts her hand from her chest and waves me away as she turns her head to the side so that I cannot see her tears. But I hear her soft words as she whispers, "Thank you for your forgiveness."

CHAPTER 3

▼

God was at His artistic best when He sculpted the hills of Bologna. There is movement in the rise and fall of the crests and valleys, so perfectly carved and polished as they rest beneath a soft blanket of clouds. The perennial silver skies sprinkle their mist over the varying tones of green, amber, and violet in the earth below, and you can't help but thank the sun for holding back and preserving itself for the fleeting summer that eventually caresses the land with a golden glow.

On Mother's Day, Enzo and I take a taxi ride up into those blessed hills. The fare is excessive because we're driving beyond the city limits, but this place is so special to me that I don't mind. I discovered this hilltop-turned-secluded-park back when I lived in this town. A co-worker had told me about it, and I had explored it one morning while I was still pregnant. My not-so-private hilltop is a grassy knoll with only a few trees and a panoramic view of the city of Bologna in one direction and the hills leading into the Apennine Mountains in the other. Unfortunately, I had never returned to this peaceful place because transport was inconvenient without a car—a poor reason to avoid a place so precious, but that was my excuse.

The taxi drops us off, and I arrange for pickup in two hours' time. The driver raises an eyebrow as he estimates the fee, but I shake my head and tell him not to worry about it. "This is a special day," I tell him as I enter the cab company's phone number into my cell phone memory, just in case.

Enzo and I are not the only ones in the park on this Sunday afternoon. May is always a splendid time in Bologna since the cold air has given way to cool, clear days. Up here on the hill, it's a bit colder than down below, but I've prepared by bringing my sweater and even one for Enzo, which Annabella grabbed for me before Enzo and I left. I have put together a picnic basket of dessert treats, and I spread out the blanket as soon as Enzo picks the spot.

He seems nervous, but I understand. I have brought some other things with me in my satchel to help pass the time, one of which is the present that I never gave him yesterday. We settle down, and I open the basket with lots of fanfare. "Ooh! Aah! Will you look at what I have here?" I pull out some mini tarts and chocolate-filled croissants. Enzo smiles and takes the tart with the slice of strawberry on top.

"*Grazie,*" he says.

"*Prego.* Enzo, did you know that today is Mother's Day in my country?"

Enzo looks up apologetically. "Yes, I'm sorry. Happy Mother's Day!"

"Thank you. I just wanted to let you know that being with you today means so much to me. I've spent too many Mother's Days without you, and I'm very sorry for that."

"Why didn't you come back?" He asks innocently but with a hint of bitterness.

"You asked me another difficult question yesterday, which I promised to answer today, didn't I?"

"Yes, you did."

I've been leaning back on my hands, but now I switch to the cross-legged position and lean closer in to Enzo. "You certainly deserve an explanation," I say, and then take the last bite of my tart.

"Yes, I do," he says confidently.

I smile as I finish chewing my tart and then proceed. "Your babbo and I got married before you were born, and after you were born, we were happy for a little while. We were thrilled to have you in our lives, but we were young and not so sure about each other. We started to disagree about many important things...the kind of things that you can't just ignore."

"Like what?" Enzo asks.

"Grown-up things," I pull out my trump card in order to avoid giving out too much information. "Anyway, I hadn't visited my family back in Miami since before I got married, and I missed them. When my father got sick, I decided to go see him. You were only two years old at that time, and I hadn't been able to get you an American passport yet, so you couldn't come with me. I really would have liked your American grandparents to meet you." I pause at this point because now comes the part where I must lie, and that pains me. Enzo is looking down, but I know that he's listening. "Once I got back to Miami, I had to stay longer than I'd planned because my father was so ill that my mother couldn't take care of him by herself. She needed my help, Enzo. Do you understand that?"

"Yes," he whispers.

"I knew that you were safe back here with Babbo and Nonna, so I felt okay staying in Miami for a while to help my parents. I never planned to stay away from you for such a long time, but then I had legal problems with the Italian government. That means that they wouldn't let me back into Italy because there was a problem with my legal papers." I hope that Enzo doesn't have the worldliness to question why I couldn't even visit. He's sitting quietly, not asking questions, so I continue. "I tried to fix the problems many times, but it never worked. But then, finally, Annabella was able to fix things for me, and now I'm here. Oh, I've missed you so much, Enzo! You have no idea."

Enzo looks up. "Why couldn't Babbo or Nonna fix things for you?"

He's a smart boy. I have promised Carlo that I won't make him the bad guy, but I will make no efforts to make him the good guy either. "I have no idea, Enzo. But I'm here with you now, and I'm not going anywhere for a very long time."

My story sounds weak and flawed to my own ears, but Enzo is taking it all in stride. Then he asks me a question that I haven't anticipated. "Do you have a new husband and other children?"

It's a fair question since Carlo has a new wife and soon a new baby. At least, I can answer this question truthfully. "No, Enzo. There is a man, who I love very much back in the United States, but we're not married, and I don't have any other children. You are my only child, and I haven't stopped thinking about you since the day I left Bologna." It takes all my effort not to cry as I talk to Enzo, and I'm doing a good job. Then I remember my satchel of surprises. "I think now is a good time to give you a present."

Enzo smiles, probably relieved that I'm lightening the mood. I pull out a wrapped package and hand it to him. "This is to let you know how much I've missed you these past years."

Enzo tears open the paper but doesn't seem to know what he has found.

"This one," I point to the leather bound book, "Is my journal. I wrote an entry in it every Sunday night before I went to bed. I hoped you would see it some day, and I wanted you to know what my life was like and how much I was thinking of you."

Enzo thumbs through the pages. "Your handwriting is messy."

"I'm sorry. I was sad a lot of the time, so I guess I didn't write so well."

Enzo picks up the other bound book. "What's this one?"

"That's a photo album. You can put pictures of whatever you'd like in there, but I have to be honest with you. I'm hoping that you'll want to put at least one picture of you and me in there so we can start making some new memories."

I pull my digital camera out of my bag and playfully wave it in the air. Enzo looks at the camera and then at me. I can almost see the gears spinning inside his head. Should he yell at me and tell me all the angry thoughts that are screaming to come out? Or should he be nice and cut his mamma some slack on Mother's Day? Apparently, Enzo is a well-raised child. He looks directly at me with a stern expression, but says, "*Va bene.*"

I look around and spot a couple only feet away on their picnic blanket. I walk over to them and ask if one of them would be so kind as to take a picture of my son and me. I smile as I ask because I love saying the words, *my son.* The woman happily obliges me and follows me back to Enzo. I sit back down next to him on our colorful blanket and smile at the camera. Before the woman can snap the photo, Enzo throws an arm around my shoulder and leans his head in closer to me. I freeze, not for the camera, but for the sensation of his touch. I never want this moment to end. The lady takes the picture and shouts, "Perfect!"

To this day, that is my favorite picture in the whole world. Perfect.

It is Sunday evening, and I'm exhausted. Enzo and I ended up hiking in the hills until almost 5:30, when my loyal taxi driver returned. I dropped Enzo back home and thanked him for the best Mother's Day ever. He hugged me and said that I was very nice and that he wanted to see me again soon. I feel so good yet so out of sorts because I don't have my journal with me anymore, and it is Sunday night. I am supposed to be writing, but I don't need to any more. Instead, I want to talk to Matthew. I want to tell him everything about my weekend with Enzo. It's just after lunchtime in New York, so I first try Matthew at home.

"Hello?"

He answers the phone, and I immediately hear a woman's voice in the background. *"Ciao*, Matthew. Do your homework. *Ci vediamo domani."* See you tomorrow. I hear Matthew's door slam, and I'm so thrown off that I look at my cell phone to see if I've dialed the right number.

"Matthew?"

"Millie! Hey, my love! How are things going?"

"Was there an Italian woman in your apartment?" I don't care about niceties right now. I want to know about the woman.

"What? No. That was the TV. So, Haley tells me that you've seen Enzo. Why didn't you call me?"

I'm frustrated that Matthew has ruined my perfect mood by lying to me, but I play the game because, at this moment, I have no other choice. "I saw him again today, and I wanted to wait to call you to tell you everything." I tell Matthew the whole story, finishing with the perfect photograph, which I promise to download from my camera as soon as possible and forward to him. "I've decided what I'm going to do tomorrow morning. Even though summer is coming, I'm going to stop in on some of my old directors and see if I can get a teaching position. They sometimes have summer courses, and if not, they'll hopefully have classes for me for the fall term."

"Sounds great. It's nice that you want to get established there and get yourself settled in." There's something odd about Matthew's tone, and I don't like it at all.

"Have you made your reservations for Christmas yet?"

"Millie, you haven't even been gone one week! Give me a chance here. I told you I'll be there, and I keep my promises."

"I love you, you know," I say.

"I know. And I love you, too…very much."

My days are going by quickly. I have three summer classes that I teach in the morning every day. They began in June and will continue until the end of July. In August, there's no business; everyone is on vacation. After my classes, I return, on foot, up Via dell'Osservanza to make myself lunch. After lunch, I make my calls to the U.S. since everyone there is just starting their day by then, and it's a good time to find them. After my phone calls, it's time to hike back down the hill and either do shopping or other errands that I have or meet Enzo for an afternoon stroll through the center. We do this almost every other day, which Annabella really likes because it gives her some time for herself.

My strolls with Enzo are educational. We talk about his school, his best friend—Daniele, the girl he likes—Alessia, and his favorite soccer team—Juventus. I have found out that Enzo has another secret passion that he doesn't like to advertise…he loves to sing. So, we spend lots of time in the music store, selecting his favorite music and always making sure that the lyrics are included in the CD jacket. If not, Enzo won't make the purchase. (I should say that he will not give me permission to make the purchase.) So far, I've bought him four CDs, and he has started greeting me with a serenade of a different song from each CD each time we meet. I love it, and I always cheer when he finishes. He inevitably reminds me that I can't tell Carlo or Annabella about it…every time. I don't know why he feels the need to keep his singing so secret, but I'm flattered that I share this with him and so honor his request. It gives me great pleasure to know that I have a piece of Enzo that Carlo does not. And given the fact that I have creatively avoided speaking to Carlo, this won't be a difficult promise to keep.

I have been in Bologna now for almost six weeks, and my phone calls with Matthew have gotten stranger and stranger. He intermittently throws out little Italian phrases, saying that he's kind of studying Italian so that he can have an easier time when he visits. Being a language professor, I don't know how one *kind of* studies a language. I remind Matthew that I'll be here to translate for him, but he just shoos me off and talks about something else, which only makes me think about the Italian girl who was in his apartment last May. I don't think that he's cheating on me, but I believe that something strange is going on. When I ask Haley about Matthew, she blows me off even worse and only reminds me of how excited Matthew is for his December trip.

"But December is so far away," I complain to Haley.

"It'll be here before you know it," she always responds.

I am tired of the same nonsensical conversations, and I feel like I have no idea of what's going on in Matthew's life. I'm frustrated and tired of the telephone. Just as I am once again cursing the phone for interfering with my conversation, it rings. I answer it and hear Carlo on the other end. "Mamma has just passed away."

"I'm so sorry, Carlo." And I am.

"She left you something, if you can believe it."

"I can't." What in God's name Regina would want to bestow upon me?

"Well, she did. Please come by this evening if you can. You can pick it up then. And I'd like to talk to you about something anyway."

I am sitting on Regina's sofa as Carlo stands before me with an envelope in his hand. "Before I give you this, you have to explain yourself to me."

I'm confused by this game. "What do you want me to explain?"

Carlo sits down beside me, resting the envelope on his lap like a prize for me to covet. "The last time you were here, you told me to search for my family in a synagogue. Why did you say that?"

Have you ever been put on the spot and decided to mentally escape when you physically couldn't? As Carlo waits for my response, I can't hear my own thoughts. *My Favorite Things* is singing in my ears, the saxophonist's lilting notes jumping up and down with each cadence.

"Millie?" Carlo leans in closer to me, demanding my focus.

I shake my head quickly and look him in the eye. "I don't know, Carlo. I guess you were right. I'm having some 'difficulties.' Now, may I please see my envelope?"

I put out my right hand, with my open palm awaiting delivery. Carlo mentally debates pressing the issue but gives in and hands me my only inheritance. I see that the outside of the envelope says, *Please mail to Emilia.* Inside I find a note and a smaller sealed envelope. I read the note first, which is difficult since it's scrawled in Italian on a piece of old stationery in very poor handwriting. It is dated April, 2005.

Dear Emilia,

I found this photograph today while sifting through some old things. If I die soon, which I think I may, I want you to have it instead of Carlo. I know that I've wronged you and there's nothing I can do to change that. But maybe this picture will clarify some things for you. You may, of course, send it back to Carlo and explain to him what it is. You can tell him that I once gave in to his father's wishes, before the Mazzini family slighted me. After I am dead, I do not care if my son thinks badly of me. I tried to be a good mamma, but I made some terrible mistakes. For that, I owe you and Carlo a big apology. I am sorry for pushing you out of Carlo and Enzo's lives, but my anger was too strong. And I'm sorry that I don't have the courage to call you and say this to you directly. Good luck to you, and may you find peace in your life, in spite of what I took from you.

Sincerely,

Regina Buonsignore di Mazzini

I open the second envelope and find a photograph of a man, woman, and infant. The man and the infant are wearing yarmulkes, and the man is sporting a proud smile as he holds the child up to show the world. I turn over the photo, and on the back is written *Enzo, Regina, and Carlo; Bologna, March 12, 1971.* The picture was taken eight days after Carlo was born. It was his *bris.* I whisper, mostly to myself, "Carlo had a *bris.*"

"What?" asks Carlo. "Can I see that?" In a dazed state, I hand Carlo the photo. "Who are these people?" He turns over the photo to read the names written in his mother's penmanship. Then he looks up at me. "I don't understand, Millie."

Annabella and Enzo have walked into the salon, and I look over at them before I explain. I don't know if Carlo wants them privy to a secret about to be exposed, so I look back at Carlo and wait for him to give me a sign.

"What's going on?" Enzo asks.

"Mamma left Millie a picture, but I don't understand it."

Carlo looks at me and waits for me to speak. When I do, I direct my words to Annabella because I am afraid of seeing Carlo's face when he finds out. "It's a picture of Carlo, Mamma, and Carlo's babbo, Enzo. It was taken when Carlo was only eight days old...at his *bris.*"

"His what?" Annabella asks.

Feeling bolder, I look at Carlo. "Your father was Jewish, Carlo. Your mamma agreed to let you be circumcised in the Jewish way when you were eight days old, as the Torah mandates. When your babbo died, your mamma felt slighted by the Mazzinis, and she cut herself off from them completely. She continued to raise you in Catholicism, without ever revealing to you your Jewish roots."

"How do you know this?" Carlo is angry and confused, understandably.

"She told my sister back in '97 when Romy came to try and fix things for me."

"You've known this since 1997?" Carlo is incredulous.

"Yes." I have no more to say.

"And you didn't tell me?" Carlo's arms are spread wide, palms facing heaven.

"You weren't answering your phone, Carlo, and you..." I look over at Enzo, suddenly remembering that he's in the room. I was about to say, *You stole my son*, but Enzo's hazel eyes fixed on mine stop me before I ruin everything that I have achieved thus far. I turn back to Carlo. "This is your mamma's way of saying she's sorry to me."

Carlo now has his head in his hands and says nothing. Then, Enzo speaks. "My nonno was Jewish?"

There's silence as I wait to see who should answer. Carlo takes my breath away when he says, "Yes, and so is your mamma."

CHAPTER 4

▼

Regina Buonsignore di Mazzini is buried on June 29, 2006, and I cry for my Enzo. He has lost his nonna, who helped raised him and helped make him the fine boy that he is today. For that, I owe her respect, and as the Latin chants fill the church, I silently recite the Hebrew Mourner's Kaddish and cry for the woman who lived with a tortured soul.

I look over at Enzo, who is seated between Carlo and Annabella. Enzo hasn't so much as looked at me all morning, and when he catches me watching him, he throws a hard glance my way. It frightens me, and I turn away quickly, pained by his angry eyes. What have I done? I came into Enzo's world and rocked the boat so hard and so quickly that I think I've created a wake too powerful to ride out. There's so much I want to say to my son, but there's apparently so little that he wants to say to me. Patience is the virtue that I must once more (and perhaps forever) exercise with my son.

Two days later is Enzo's eleventh birthday, which, of course, is followed by my thirty-fourth. On Saturday, July first, I'm pleasantly surprised to be invited to Enzo's birthday party at the park, though I'm well aware of the distance between Enzo and me. I feel like one of the grown up guests who Enzo doesn't know and doesn't care to know, which is a frightening feeling given the ground we've covered since my arrival. Regina's post mortem revelation hasn't quite turned out the way I would have hoped. Enzo keeps me beyond arm's length, and Carlo looks at me as if I've aired laundry too dirty to be washed. Annabella is the only person who isn't punishing me, but her detachment ever since my reunion with Enzo has also been apparent. And why not? She's done her job and has her own issues to manage. The bottom line is that I feel more alone than ever, and at moments I even wish I could take back the words I spoke and leave them resting on the paper, sealed in an envelope forever. How long can they go on punishing me? I wasn't the one who created the secret, simply the one who quenched its burning power.

As I observe those around me, I decide to view the past days' happenings as nothing more than an unfortunate setback. The kids have engaged in a soccer game while the adults sip cappuccino, beer, or wine. I initiate small talk with Alessia's mother, and the woman asks where in the States I am from. I tell her, and she asks me how I know the Mazzinis. It's an awkward moment, but I knew this time would eventually come. I smile proudly. "I'm Enzo's mamma."

Alessia's mother looks at me blankly. "I'm sorry, but I thought Enzo's mamma was dead."

At this, I look the woman squarely in the eye, shocked at how little tact she has, but then recover. "Well, I had to pull a lot of strings," I look up to Heaven. "And God gave me another chance." It is not a complete lie.

Carlo can't stand the idea of cleaning out his mamma's things, and so Annabella and I have taken on the task on the eve of my birthday—a lovely way to spend a Saturday night. At first, Carlo was put out that I would be rummaging through Regina's personal items, but he didn't put up much of a fight when I suggested that I might find a plethora of secrets waiting to be disclosed. He just shooed me away, saying, "I hope you find the Holy Grail." Carlo could never have predicted the power of his snide remark, for as I unpack the one box hidden beneath a mound of old coats, what I discover is as close to the Holy Grail as I could hope for.

In a worn leather binder with cracked edges (something straight out of an archive museum) is a packet of documents—a mixture of sealed certificates and handwritten letters in a woman's pretty penmanship. I ask Annabella's permission to review the papers, not wanting to trespass where uninvited, and when she nods her head without looking my way, I carefully separate the pages and begin to read. As I peruse birth certificates and casually written notes, I realize that I have indeed stumbled upon a library, in miniature, of Regina's secret family history.

Marrano Jews were Spanish and Portuguese conversos, many of whom fled Iberia and headed for Italy as early as 1492 and continued to do so into the sixteenth century. Many Marranos were received by the ports of Ancona and Pesaro, two small cities whose economies flourished with the arrival of the expelled refugees. In addition, Marranos settled in better-known cities such as Florence, Venice, Naples, and Rome, as well as other lesser-known towns such as Bologna. Despite renewed persecution in 1556 from Pope Paul IV, many of the Marranos managed to avoid imprisonment and survive into the modern era. Some openly resumed the once hidden practice of Judaism, while others continued as Christians, too afraid to reopen old wounds.

From what I can glean, Regina's maternal line was made up of Marranos who not only refused to openly declare their Judaism, but who chose to suppress it in an attempt to wipe it out completely. It seems that Regina's mother, Adina Cagliari, was the one who discovered her hidden bloodline and had tried to salvage as much documentation as she could to preserve her family's heritage. As history has proven time and again, Jewish culture dies hard, and Adina wasn't going down without a fight.

I say nothing as I read through the evidence. Annabella stands up, wiping dusty hands off on her maternity jeans, and mumbles something about going to get some garbage bags to pack up this trash. I am breathless as I stare at the treasure before me, asking myself countless questions. Why did Regina keep this archive? Was it her attempt at honoring her past? Did Enzo Mazzini Sr. know about his wife's Jewish heritage? Did Regina even know what secrets the box contained? Maybe she had never read its contents but had made a promise to her mother to preserve the carton.

I will never know Regina's motivation for keeping this box since she is no longer around to bear the burden of her secrets. But there is one conclusion I have reached. Regina Buonsignore di Mazzini wore her role of the self-pitying victim of one Jewish family's intolerance so well that it became a security blanket—comforting in times of self-doubt but too heavy to shed even when the underlying layers of her past made life too hot to bear.

Annabella returns to the closet, where I am still seated on the floor, my latest revelation displayed openly before me. "What's all that?" she asks.

I look up at her, weighing the strength of my position in this family. "It's Regina's family history." Annabella slowly bends down to sit by my side. "But it's not a story that Carlo will like to hear," I tell her.

Annabella and I look at each other, our eyes no more than eighteen inches apart. She speaks to me in a soft but meaningful tone. "Why don't you gather up those papers and keep them somewhere safe. Maybe they'll be useful some day…for Enzo."

I nod once and smile at my son's step-mother. I am grateful that he has such a compassionate woman in his life, and I tell her so in two words that I whisper so softly that I can hardly hear myself. "Thank you."

On Sunday, my director (Annabella's mother and Enzo's step-grandmother) hosts a lunch at her house for my birthday. Carlo obviously doesn't love the idea of spending his whole weekend with me, but he has no choice but to accept the unfortunate coincidence that his child and the mother of his child virtually share a birthday. In contrast to Carlo, I am in heaven spending so much time around Enzo. If Carlo weren't there, the picture would be perfect, but I have reached acceptance. In fact, I don't even notice Carlo's presence most of the time. It's curious to me how easily this man disappears into the woodwork when I'm around. Does he behave differently around me, or have I just gotten so used to not having him in my life that I don't even see him any more?

As for Enzo, I have no idea how long he can hold his grudge, so I decide to face my son with confidence, as I imagine a good mother would do. When most of the guests have left and the party is coming to a close, I pull Enzo into a bedroom. "I miss you," I say.

He smiles weakly.

"I'd like to share something with you," I show Enzo my cell phone. "You know how I talk about a man named Matthew a lot?"

"Yes."

"Since it's my birthday, I'd like to talk to him. I'd like you to say hello if you're comfortable with that. He's heard so much about you."

Enzo thinks about it a moment and then nods his head. "*Va be'.*"

I phone Matthew, praying that he'll be home, and when he answers, I light up. "Wish me a Happy Birthday!" I say happily.

"Happy Birthday, Beautiful! How are you?"

"Great!" I smile at Enzo. "I'm having a fabulous birthday weekend with Enzo. Speaking of whom, he's standing right next to me. Would you like to say hello?"

"*Va bene,*" Matthew says, and I get that queasy feeling again.

Still, I hand the phone to Enzo, and I sit down on the bed and watch my son talk to Matthew. I am full of mixed emotions. I am warmed to the core that the two most important men in my life are connecting, yet I am sickened by the idea that Matthew could be pulling the wool over my eyes as I blindly go about my personal business. I want them to meet each other so badly, yet I am afraid that such a meeting may never happen.

Enzo finally says good-bye and hands me the phone.

"Matthew?" I check to see that he is still there.

"I'm here. Enzo sounds great, Millie."

"Yeah. Can I call you to chat more later, when I'm back home? I have so much to tell you." I hope I don't sound as desperate as I suddenly feel.

"Actually, Millie, I'm going out with Haley and Adam in a bit, so I won't be around until it's too late. So Happy Birthday again, my love!"

I hang up the phone and stare at it as if I have never seen a cell phone before. Why doesn't Matthew realize how important this birthday is for me? I have so much to tell him about my weekend, but he has other things to do that don't involve me.

As I'm falling into my world of me, Enzo interrupts. "Why was it a big secret that you're Jewish?"

I literally shake my head to clear out the demons and be able to concentrate on Enzo's question. "I was wondering when you were going to ask me about that?" I am relieved that he is finally bridging the gap between us, and I try to smile as I bide my time looking for the appropriate response.

"I've never known Jewish people before," Enzo simply says.

"Yes, well, I think that's part of the problem."

Enzo patiently waits for me to say more.

"You know, Enzo, that nobody is perfect. Well, your nonna made a mistake. When she was younger, she felt very hurt by your nonno's family, and they were Jewish. So, she made the mistake of believing that because they had hurt her and they were Jewish that all Jewish people were bad. Do you understand?"

He nods slowly.

"So Nonna didn't want anyone to know that she had Jewish people in her family, and she didn't like me very much because I'm Jewish."

"Did you do anything mean to her?" It's a logical question. If Jews had hurt her before, my innocent boy wants to know if I had also hurt his nonna.

"I don't think that I was mean to her, Enzo. I tried my best to be kind and respectful because I loved your babbo."

"Did Babbo love you?" My son is not going to make this easy for me.

"I think he did, but that changed. And that part of the story is something we can discuss when you're a lot older." I have to nip this in the bud.

"I don't care that you're Jewish," Enzo says.

"Thank you." I'm not sure if I want to continue this discussion right now.

Then, much to my relief, Enzo changes the direction of our talk. "How long are you going to be in Bologna?"

"Do you want me to leave already?" I smile playfully.

"No. I like you."

I am moved, and I pat the spot on the bed next to me for Enzo to sit down. He follows my cue. "Before I answer your question, Enzo, may I ask you one?"

"*Va be'.*"

"Back in May, when you first met me, you said that you kind of remembered me. What did you mean?"

Enzo looks up to the ceiling. "There's a dream I had. Well, I don't really know if it's a dream or a memory, but I like to think of it when I'm by myself. I'm in a shower, and the warm water is pouring all over me. Someone else is in the shower with me, but I'm covered in so many bubbles that I can't see the person. I feel so happy when I think about being covered in so many bubbles, like I'm a cloud that can float away if I want." Enzo notices that I am silently crying. "I like to pretend that the person in the shower is my mamma who left, because that would make the memory perfect. When I saw you in the park, I thought of my dream, and I thought that maybe you were the person in the shower."

I am crying harder.

"Were you?" Enzo's little face has tightened up as he tries to hold back his own tears. I nod my head strongly because I have no breath to speak. I'm still nodding when he leans forward and hugs me tightly, letting his tears flow like a warm shower pouring over us both. Enzo and I remain locked in our hug for a long moment before he pulls away and asks me again. "How long will you be here?"

I wipe my eyes and smile at my boy, who seems to want me to stay. "My plan is to stay here for the whole year, until next summer. I'm on a kind of really long vacation from work, but eventually my vacation will end. So, next summer, we'll see how things are going for you and me, and I can make a decision about where we'll go from there."

"So, you might go back to Miami forever?" Enzo is worried.

"Enzo, if I decide to go back to Miami, it will be because I feel so secure in my relationship with you that I believe you can finish your schooling here with Babbo and Annabella but come visit me on all your vacations. Or I'll come visit you!"

"And what if I don't want you to leave?" Enzo wears a very serious expression as he poses that possibility to me.

"I will be overjoyed, and we'll cross that bridge when we get to it."

Then my son says something that seems out of place and takes me off guard. "I'm having mean thoughts about Nonna, and I don't like that. Would you take me to church tomorrow so I can confess my sins?"

A small gasp escapes me. It is a long road to travel between Enzo's semantic understanding and intellectual understanding of the fact that I'm Jewish, and I am quickly reminded of the journey that he and I have yet to make. But right here, at this moment on my birthday, I know it's not the time to embark on that journey because this is not about me. My little boy needs me to comfort him in the only way he has ever known. I nod my head. "Of course I'll take you, Enzo, but I hope you know that it's okay to feel whatever you need to feel."

He looks confused, and I realize that, in Enzo's world, words of forgiveness can only be administered by a priest.

"I do miss Nonna, you know."

"I know," I say. Then I realize why Enzo is so concerned about my leaving. It takes everything that I'm made of to speak highly of Regina, but I do. "Your nonna took great care of you, and you were very lucky to have her in your life. But Nonna died because she was very sick, and I'd like to believe that she's happier now to be feeling better in Heaven than she did here on Earth."

Enzo nods in agreement.

"I promise you, Enzo, that I will *never* abandon you again. If I return to Miami, it will be with your permission."

He looks at me with a tilted head.

"I know that I probably haven't earned your trust yet, but I hope that I will soon so that you'll see how much I love you and how much I want to be a part of your life."

There is a moment of silence as Enzo takes it all in. Then he hugs me again and softly says words that I thought I would never hear, "*Ti voglio bene, Mamma.*" I love you, Mommy.

CHAPTER 5

▼

July 4, 2006, American Independence Day, but here in Italy, it's just another steamy summer Tuesday. Today reminds me of last year's Independence Day when Matthew announced his break up with Rachel, and that makes me want to call him to wish him a happy day. I look at my watch and see that it's too early to call New York, especially on a holiday, so I set the alarm on my cell phone to remind me to call Matthew this evening.

When my alarm sounds at nine o'clock, I dial Matthew's number but get his voice mail, so I immediately enter the number for his cell phone. It rings several times before he picks up. "Hello?"

I hear lots of background noise and what sound like announcements coming over a public announcement system. "Where are you?" I ask him.

"Millie! I'm...I'm...I'm at an event...in the park." He's such a bad liar. "What's up?"

"I just wanted to wish you Happy Independence Day...like last year."

"Oh, right. Thanks! Are you doing anything to celebrate?"

"I'm in Italy, Matthew. They don't celebrate America's independence from the British."

Matthew laughs awkwardly. "Right. Listen, Millie. I've got to go. There's a...thing going on, and they're waiting for me. I love you!"

Matthew is such a bad liar.

Last night was a waste of my living. I actually sat alone in my beautiful cottage and got drunk on cheap red wine, the kind that comes in a carton instead of a bottle. I usually use that type of wine for cooking, but I wanted to drink and it was all I had. My phone conversation with Matthew left me even more tortured than I had felt after my birthday phone call. I tormented my brain by imagining stories with too many missing pieces, creating a frustrating feeling of emptiness and misdirected anger. I was angry at Matthew for potentially deceiving me, especially since I believe that it goes completely against his grain. I was angry at Regina for dying her way out of a true confession and putting the burden on me—a burden that I will probably carry with me until Enzo is old enough to see the bigger picture. I was angry at Carlo for still not being man enough to acknowledge his crime or beg my forgiveness. I was angry at myself for feeling so angry.

The only person who I wasn't angry at was Enzo, the innocent boy who has made it through nine years with Carlo and Regina and who appears to have survived unscathed. He could have easily turned out to be a bitter and insecure child who wanted nothing more than to throw slanderous remarks my way or deny me so much as a smile. Instead, Enzo has an open heart and the patience of Job, a character trait that my own mother admired in me for so many years.

I drank nearly a liter last night, which means that I woke up this morning with a pounding headache and a terrible taste in my mouth. I would like to erase the last eighteen hours from the pages of the Book of Life, to which my father always likes to refer when we do things that are stupid or ridiculous.

"Be careful!" He'll say. "That's being inscribed in the Book of Life, and God is shaking his head as he reads it."

We all usually laugh to realize how silly it will look to read those pages when we get up to Heaven.

It is now the late afternoon on July fifth, and I am once more seated on the steps of the San Petronio Basilica in Piazza Maggiore. Compared to this morning, I feel better physically but not emotionally. I'm not as angry any more as much as I am lonely, and I won't be able to see Enzo for a couple of weeks because he has gone on a short holiday with Carlo and Annabella's family, who has a vacation home in the Dolomites, part of the Alpine Mountain Range, where they love to spend the hottest and the coldest months of the year.

Piazza Maggiore is quiet today, so I decide to head home and enjoy the strenuous walk up Via dell'Osservanza. As I leave the piazza, I head up Via D'Azelio and find the side street that houses the apartment where Carlo, Enzo, and I lived together and where Michela and I lived before that. As miserable as those times often were, I miss them, and I wonder what has become of Michela. It's amazing how our minds protect us by rose-coloring our memories, and when I look at the building, I say out loud, "I loved that place."

I continue heading up D'Azelio to Porto San Mamolo, the entrance to the Viale. I cross the busy boulevard, walk one block to Via dell'Osservanza, and turn right to begin my steep, kilometer-long ascent. That part of the walk alone takes fifteen minutes, which are the prettiest fifteen minutes of my day.

When I am about half-way up Osservanza, a taxi comes chugging up the hill, and its fumes send me into a brief coughing fit. I glance quickly into the cab and see a man seated in the back, looking out at me with a frightened look on his face. I could swear that it's Matthew. I immediately feel very angry that my insecurity about him is causing me to conjure up his image in the first stranger I see, and I start cursing to no one but the trees.

As I approach the fourteenth Station of the Cross, I notice that the taxi had stopped in front of my gate but has now turned around to head back down the hill. I assume that the cabbie's fare is visiting Villa Aldini, and I think nothing of it. Then, I round the bushes that block my gate from street view, and there he is.

Matthew Crane is standing at my front door, flanked by a large, rolling suitcase and a small backpack. He sees me coming and throws his arms open wide. "*Ciao, Bella!*"

My knees get weak as things start to spin. My world is full of perfect turmoil as the heat engulfs me and I fall to the ground. The last thing I remember before fainting is Matthew yelling, "Holy Shit!"

Fortunately, I fell where there was a small patch of grass before the driveway begins, and my head was smart enough to choose to land on green instead of gray. I awake a few moments later to see many people looking over me. Matthew is holding a cool, wet towel over my forehead, and my landlady is fanning my face with a magazine. Three unknown onlookers are standing near my feet, mumbling in Italian. When I open my eyes, Matthew gets excited. "Millie!"

"Emilia!" Shouts my landlady. "Are you all right?"

I try to nod my head, but it hurts in the back and on the right side. I move my hand to the pain and then pull it away to look for blood.

"Just a few small spots," Matthew says as he takes my hand in his and surveys what I have found. "Can you move your neck, Millie?"

I can, and I try to sit up. "Yeah, I'm okay." I realize that I've got road burn on my right elbow and lower arm, my spine, and the back of my right calf. "I need to get cleaned up."

The onlookers disperse as Matthew and my landlady help me to my feet and into my house. I notice Matthew's bags still outside the front door, and I realize that he couldn't get in because I have the key.

"It's a good thing I got home when I did," comments my landlady.

"*Mille grazie.*" Matthew thanks her, and my head begins to spin again at the sound of Italian pouring from his lips.

Matthew helps me into the salon and sits me down on the sofa. "I'm getting you a glass of water and an ice pack. Don't move!" As he walks to the kitchen he yells, "Boy, Millie! You really know how to steal my thunder!"

When Matthew returns to the salon, I say, "A little warning would have been nice."

"Ah, but that wouldn't have been as much fun." Then he surveys my head wound and changes his mind. "I guess I've still got it. At thirty-one years old, I can still make the girls swoon."

I cannot help but smile.

"You don't need any stitches. It's already stopped bleeding. The bad news is that I have to keep you awake for quite a while now, so don't even think about taking a nap."

"Yes, Doctor," I say and then add, "What in God's name are you doing here?"

Matthew sits down next to me on the sofa. "I thought you'd never ask."

It appears that while I had been busy planning my Italian return and then living *la bella vita*, Matthew has been stirring his own brew. Back in March, when Haley and Adam got married, Matthew realized that things were happening that were out of his control, namely my reunion with Enzo. Watching Haley swear eternal love to Adam moved Matthew to consider how he would feel to lose me yet again. He decided that he couldn't let that happen.

Upon returning to New York, he began inquiring about professional opportunities in Bologna and was pleasantly surprised to discover that Rizzoli is not a small village but rather a European renowned, orthopedic hospital and research center, formally called the Istituto Ortopedici Rizzoli. He mentioned the institute to his boss, who guided Matthew on how to search for possible research grants overseas. With Rizzoli's excellent reputation, it was apparently not so difficult for Matthew to find a match with an American orthopedic implant company that was already contracted with the institute to analyze a potential new product. Matthew immediately began his Italian classes at his local community school in May upon receiving confirmation of his acceptance as a research engineer. The position starts in mid-July, which is why Matthew is sitting on my sofa here in Bologna, holding an ice pack against my head and periodically checking my pulse.

All the pieces come together like an annoying puzzle that I just couldn't solve and had become rather fed up working on. As for the day I called Matthew and heard an Italian woman's voice, his instructor had stopped by to drop off a book that he had left in class the week before. As for yesterday's July Fourth blow off, Matthew was in Miami International Airport, awaiting his flight to Italy.

"All this time," I tell Matthew, "I thought you were such a bad liar, but you're actually quite good at it."

He laughs.

"But I think you've had enough practice for now, so let's leave the lies alone for a while, *va bene?*"

Matthew kisses me and removes the ice from my head. "I have a very important question for you, Millie."

"Shoot."

"Can I live here with you?"

Is he for real? Did he really make all these plans, find a job, fly across the ocean to a foreign land, and casually forget to arrange for living accommodations? Or did he know that I would never let him live anywhere else? I look at my boyfriend with a poker face. "You can stay in the guest bedroom."

Now, *he* looks like the one who might faint, and I feel bad for him.

"You must be exhausted," I say. I stand up, take Matthew's hand, and lead him upstairs to my room. "This is our bedroom." I throw open the door to find the late afternoon sunlight splashing over the white linens. Matthew is still speechless. "I know I'm not supposed to fall asleep, but am I allowed to recline in bed?"

I smile flirtatiously as my senses completely return. My fall in the street feels like hours ago, and I look at Matthew. I feel grateful for the wonders of my life and the blessing of timing. Matthew leads me to our bed, and we spend the next two weeks enjoying our privacy and getting to know each other again.

When Enzo returns from the North, I am sure that I will once again be filled with the awe-inspiring emotions that God has recently bestowed upon me. For all my years of private suffering and irrevocable loss, I have apparently kept my karma clean because things are finally going my way.

Where will my future take me? Back to Miami, or to a new life in Bologna? I have no idea. But I have love, I have a newfound understanding of all that has transpired, and I have Enzo.

978-0-595-40782-8
0-595-40782-X

Printed in the United States
59239LVS00001B/37-60